The Pick Up

Fiona Donovan

To order additional copies of this book, contact:
Xlibris Corporation
1-888-795-4274
www.Xlibris.com
Orders@Xlibris.com
125842

PROLOGUE

I slowly stir out of the mind-numbing stupor that I had allowed myself to fall into to realize how very quiet it has become. No insect noises coming through the window down the hall, no voices or laughter, no feet shuffling around on the dusty wood floor. Unusually quiet, eerily quiet, not a sound.

Silence.

The silence captures my attention. I am now fully alert.

Straining to listen, I hear the occasional faint grunts, groans, belches, and snoring of people sleeping in the next room. They have partied themselves into a drunken stupor. My battered body is hog-tied, and I have been thrown on the filthy wooden floor in the darkened room. The reek of old death and years of filth emanates from the stained floor inches from my face. The bugs continue to dine on my skin, the relentless smothering heat weighing like a wet wool blanket over my body. Being exhausted from the constant beatings makes it nearly impossible to move into a better position to see my surroundings. Although at this point, I didn't really care anymore.

The light cast from another room down the hall makes it possible for me to barely make out the silhouette of the man standing guard inside the front door. An AK-47 casually slung over his shoulder.

I jolt as a loud crack hits the front door; it explodes open as the guard drops dead to the floor. Automatic gunfire explodes all around me. In the darkness, the muzzle flashes, and earsplitting noise from the AK-47s makes it confusing as to who was shooting whom. There is screaming and shouting in Spanish, the sound of people scurrying around trying to dodge the bullets, the alcohol making their reactions and senses slow. Among the riot of noise, I see this guy coming toward me. He looks like a Delta Force mercenary motherfucker dressed all in black, including his face, so I started to shout as loud as I could. "I'm the American rich kid! I'm the prize. I'm the American rich kid. I'm the prize. I'm the prize."

As he unties me, he says, "You don't look like a prize."

"I don't feel like one."

He drags me to my feet and starts to drag me to the front door. Among all the chaos, my heart stutters a few beats as I see the woman come running around the corner and pause. "Wait, no, wa . . ." My words die in my throat as she is gunned down. As her body crumples to the floor, I count at least six bullet holes slowly making their bloody marks on her clothes. I couldn't do anything to stop it. I can't believe it. She shouldn't have been shot. She was kind to me. I am gutted. But it is too late; she is already gone. I want to go over to her and make a move toward where she is now lying. The guy who has a hold of me pulls me away, shouting, "Come on, man, we've gotta get out of here. now!"

Once outside, I am pulled into the bed of some old pickup truck. Barely giving us time to hit the bed of the truck, the driver guns the engine, wheels screeching as we tear down the road. Just as I was about to get my bearings back, the truck swerves into this open field area where there is a chopper waiting. The blades are in motion, the pilot frantically waving us over. I am half carried, half dragged across the ground and more or less thrown into the chopper. Immediately we become airborne.

Everything happens lightning quick, the whole operation lasting maybe five minutes from the time the door blew open to my landing in the chopper.

I lie where I landed, trying to catch up in my mind.

The pilot turns to me and says, "You must know some very important people. We went through a lot to get you out."

I finally let myself give in to the black edges of unconsciousness as they move in.

CHAPTER 1

September 1979

I'm going to tell you a story. One that is mine. One that still gives me nightmares to this day.

It was a dreary Sunday morning in a quiet little neighborhood somewhere in North Central Massachusetts. I was sitting at the kitchen table in my small but simple apartment. As I sipped my coffee, I opened yesterday's *New York Times* to the classified section, personal ads, and began to scan the columns. Two-thirds of the way down the third column was something that caught my attention.

There it sat, quite simple and to the point.

It was a message meant for me. A message that demanded an answer. I had five days to do so.

I had the 1-800 number memorized. All I had to do was call it.

My curiosity getting the better of me, I dialed the number. It rang and rang and rang. I knew who would answer. It was a dedicated secure line that went directly to them. That certain someone on the other end picked up.

"Uncle John, it's John."

"Johnny Boy. Nice to hear from you."

"There's an assignment?"

"Yes, I have a pickup I need you to assist with."

"A pickup?"

"Yes, a pickup."

"O-kaay."

I was immediately suspicious. A "pickup" wasn't what I did.

I am an independent contract killer. I work for the CIA.

My suspicions caused me to wonder just what this assignment entailed and the reason for the sudden change.

My paranoia stemmed from the fact that two months previously, I had gone on a six-week trip around Europe and took vengeance on a certain assassin who had killed a very dear friend and colleague of mine. Her name was Marylyn; she shouldn't have died.

So because of my unscheduled trip off the reservation, as they say, I was regarded as highly dangerous and unpredictable. I had let my emotions become involved with a difficult situation, and that just was not tolerated by the CIA. I was now regarded as a liability.

I had a sneaky feeling that this could well be a setup to eliminate me.

CHAPTER 2

Despite all the warning sirens screaming in my head, I knew that I would accept the assignment, but it didn't stop the uneasy feeling I had about the whole thing. My conscience kept telling me, *Not a pickup, a setup.*

I was young and cocky and felt that I was somewhat invincible. My success in previous assignments just helped to solidify to me that I *was* good at what I did.

I decided I needed to call someone to bounce this off them and to get their input.

So I called one of my close colleagues, Driesdale, whom I trusted completely.

"Hey, it's John."

"Hello, John, how are you?"

"I've heard from Uncle John."

"Oh? What did he have to say?"

"There's an assignment."

"Who are on the team?"

"There's no team. It's a pickup."

"Did I hear you say 'a pickup'?"

"Yes. I have a very uneasy feeling about this one."

"You don't have to accept it."

"I know."

"John, pickups aren't your thing."

"I know. I'm thinking that this may well be a setup. Their way of paying me back for the Grueber thing."

"You could well be right. It does have that kind of feel to it. I would caution you and ask you to take your time before giving them your answer."

"Yeah," I said on a long sigh.

"I get the feeling that you have, however, already made your decision."

"I believe that I have."

"Well then, all I can say is good luck, John, and to please be careful."

As I put down the phone, I didn't feel any more reassured. My uneasiness remained the same.

I spent a sleepless night thinking about all the what-ifs of the assignment. By morning, I'd worked up a pretty good knot of anxiety that weighed heavy in my stomach. Finally, I thought, *To hell with it, what happens, happens. It should be a quick assignment anyway.*

I called Uncle John to accept the assignment. I was told that everyone would be meeting ten days from now at Ricky's house. My destination, El Salvador, Central America.

Ricky is our contact for all our Central and South American assignments. He has a vast network of contacts, so he knows a lot of people and knows where and how to obtain certain items. He ensures that we have everything we need to function and complete the assignment.

It is policy that when on assignment, it is always best to not advertise the fact that we are American. Ricky buys our clothes, toiletries, shoes and obtains any documentation and currency that we will need. He also makes hotel reservations, provides the transport, is the tour guide and the person who provides our weapons. He is known as Ricardo when he is being our guide.

I had ten days in which to put my life on hold as they say. During this time, I would make preparations for my absence. I don't know about my colleagues, but I always anticipate being gone for at least three months. Most of the time, I am back way before then.

I saw the landlord and paid him three months' rent in advance and told him that I was going away on business and if he would please keep an eye on my apartment. Fred Daniels is a kind old man. He has such a gentle and trusting way about him but will stand for no nonsense from anyone. Being retired from the Boston Police Department, he keeps himself to himself and just wants to enjoy a quiet life. He likes tenants like me who don't give him any problems and who pay their rent on time and generally mind their own business.

I methodically worked down my list of things to do, paying off any outstanding bills, paying my utilities for three months in advance, and stopping my mail delivery for the time that I was going to be gone. It made life a little less complicated this way.

By the end of the ninth day, my overnight bag was packed and sitting by the door. I packed light as I wouldn't be using anything of mine once I was in El Salvador.

CHAPTER 3

The assignment in El Salvador was an atypical one. By the time I reached the Camalapa Airport, all the details and arrangements would be taken care of by Ricardo and would take between one to two days to complete. A simple assignment.

It was not without its dangers and risks. A pickup is an exchange of money from the drug lords to the CIA. It is common knowledge that the CIA accepted monetary gifts from the drug cartels in exchange for the CIA to turn a blind eye, therefore allowing them to continue their many illegal operations. The money is then used to fund small operations within the CIA.

My role was to be a minor one in this assignment. I was simply along as a representative of the CIA, showing our good faith and trust in the drug cartels of Central and South America.

It's policy to make a habit not to fly directly to our destinations but to take extra flights to try to throw any interested parties off our intended destination.

The internal domestic flights went without problems. The flight into Mexico City, however, left me a little shaken up and unsteady. I'm not a good flyer. I do okay with the large airlines, but I have a big fear and aversion to the small planes. I am always convinced that we will crash and die. This flight was always aboard a DC3, which was a relic from World War II, and it made me uneasy and doubtful as to its flying ability. It was far from the major airlines that I had already traveled with, none of the in-flight comforts on this baby. I shared space with various pieces of cargo. It was more like riding in an industrial dryer being towed down a dirt road. The flight was extremely loud and bumpy, to say the least, and my stomach rolled every time we came across turbulence.

It was with great dread that I boarded my next flight, which would take me into Camalapa Airport, El Salvador.

This poor excuse for a plane didn't even look like it could fly. A two-seater, single-prop-engine rust bucket, probably held together with duct tape, elastic bands, and many prayers. It had more rust on the body work than paint, a big spiderweb crack in the windshield, along with various other dents, scrapes, and unidentifiable patches that looked suspiciously like Bondo. I was supposed to put my trust in this thing to get me to my destination. It was a hard sell.

I was strapped into my tiny jump seat, no bigger than a metal folding chair, my knees close to my chest and touching the back of the pilot's seat. There was poor air circulation in the cramped cockpit. The pilot's sour body odor mixing with his alcohol-laden breath added to the stifling, oppressive hot air that I had to breathe in. My stomach was already queasy and had a tight knot in it. I had already sweat through my shirt, which now clung to me like a second skin.

I sat holding on to the sides of my seat with a knuckle-whitening grip, my teeth tightly clenched. I offered up silent prayers for a safe journey as the pilot gently coaxed the engine to turn over and splutter into life. I remained that way, squeezing my eyes tightly shut all the way to El Salvador.

CHAPTER 4

When we stopped bouncing along the small runway, finally coming to a stop, I was relieved to see Ricardo waiting for me. He had what he hoped was a smile on his face, but it looked to me more like a shit-eating grin. He knew how I hated small aircraft. The '62 Chevy that he stood next to looked like the twin to the rust bucket I'd just flown in. It felt good to stand on firm ground again, my body still vibrating from the flight. My hands and jaw ached from being clamped in the same position for the duration of the flight.

The interior of the car was a little better, not quite as beat-up. I settled into the passenger seat, adjusting it slightly to accommodate my body.

The heat at once engulfed me, forcing itself onto my body. Once we were on the move, it did feel slightly better as the breeze coming in through the open windows felt cooler. The breeze carried the constant odor of rotting vegetation and dead animals in various phases of decay. The flies were relentless and extremely annoying. I looked like someone who was afflicted with a body tic as I constantly swatted at the flies.

As I sank back and started to relax a little, I started to refocus my mind back to the job at hand. It still didn't make sense, but I was here now, wasn't I?

We took Route 35, a dirt road that would take us to San Salvador, the capital. We would then pick up Route 11, the main road to Santa Ana. All roads were dirt and badly in need of a regrading. The ride was a little rough to say the least.

Our destination was a small village on the outskirts of Santa Ana. The drive would take us about two hours and was roughly eighty to one hundred miles.

There wasn't much to see along the way. The lush, rich green foliage seemed to get denser the farther we traveled. I wasn't really looking at the scenery, so no details really registered in my brain. It all looked the same to me. I believe that we passed a couple of volcanoes off in the distance, the odd crop field, but mostly I remember the tropical growth encroaching on the sides of the dirt road.

There wasn't much conversation as the roaring from the hot dusty air rushing in through the windows made it impossible to hear anything.

Ricardo did manage to tell me that I was going to be staying in the small village of El Mora, which was only ten minutes from the city of Santa Ana.

Santa Ana was where I would meet with the rest of the team and get final arrangements for the pickup.

CHAPTER 5

El Mora was more of a clearing in the tropical growth rather than what I would call a village. It had a small cluster of buildings that were identical to one another. Dirty-white stucco and wood walls with rusting tin roofs. There was no way to identify what each building was, but in such a small settlement, I guess it's not all that important. Chickens were busily scratching and pecking the dirt; somewhere, I heard a goat bleat out, and a tired-sounding cow let out a moo.

Two elderly looking men sat on wooden chairs in the shade of one of the buildings, the door wide open, kitchen sounds drifting out of the open door. Ricardo nodded his head in that general direction, acknowledged the two men with a quick wave, and told me it was the village's only cantina. Decent food, cold beer. Good to know.

As I got out of the car, I stretched and looked around. Ricardo handed me a duffel bag that he took out of the trunk. Mine remained where I had thrown it on the backseat.

The man behind the desk of the little motel looked ancient, his eyes bloodshot, greasy stringy hair pulled back into a loose ponytail, wearing a tattered, stained T-shirt. He greeted me with a smile full of rotten and broken teeth, the odor of stale sweat and beer emanating from him.

I told him that I had a reservation. He continued to stand smiling and shrugged.

"Pay US dollar, get key."

I handed over the cash that Ricardo had given me and took the key dangling from his grimy hand.

"Upstairs, second room."

I nodded and thanked him. I climbed the stairs, walked down the narrow dimly lit hallway to the second room. I opened the door onto a well-worn, tired-looking room that looked pretty clean. The sagging mattress had seen better days and, apparently, a lot of action as I could see the springs poking through the tissue-thin once-white sheets. The ceiling fan was idly turning its droopy dust-laden blades while protesting noisily with its constant *chakka, chakka, chakka, chakka.*

I took inventory of the room: bed, lopsided three-drawer dresser, nightstand, wooden chair. Bathroom: shower-tub combo, sink, mirror, toilet, towel hanging from rail. Basic, but suitable for the short time that I would be needing it.

I dropped the duffel bag onto the bed and looked around. Somewhere in this room was a message giving me the details of the meeting in Santa Ana.

I went into the bathroom, took the toilet roll from its holder. Inside the cardboard insert was a small scrap of brown paper. I took it out and replaced the toilet roll.

Tomorrow. 5:00 p.m. La Quinta Cantina. Wear red.

I tore the scrap of paper up and flushed it, then walked back to the bed and started to unpack the duffel bag. Inside I found a wallet with ID and more currency, a 9 mm Beretta with three loaded clips, basic toiletries, and a couple changes of clothes and a red shirt. There was also a small empty nylon bag meant for the clothes and items that I was currently wearing. I was to give it all to Ricardo tomorrow when he picked me up to take me to Santa Ana.

CHAPTER 6

Placing the Beretta in the back of my waistband, my wallet in my pocket, I exited the room, locking the door behind me. I wasn't planning on being gone long; I needed to eat. I made my way to the little cantina that Ricardo had pointed out to me earlier. The two elderly men no longer sat outside. I walked in through the open door, pausing to allow my eyes to adjust to the dimness inside. *Probably intentional to hide the filth and cockroaches.* There were a few small tables with mismatched chairs, the bar straight ahead. I was the only one in there other than the bartender, who was casually slouched on the bar. He stood up when he saw me enter, casually pretending to be busy wiping the counter with the most disgusting rag I had ever seen. His looks were nondescript, could be any one of a thousand Latino males. He was short, wore a toothless grin on his face, and his tattered, filthy T-shirt matched the rag in his hand.

No health inspectors in this part of the country!

I nodded acknowledgment. "Buenos noches."

"Senor. Americano?"

I nodded yes, then asked, "Alimento, cerveza?"

Nodding in the direction of the tables, he said, "*Si.* Sit. I bring."

The beer was actually cold; the plate of chicken, rice, beans, and vegetables was also pretty good. I ate quickly and quietly, keeping my head down, and left for my room as soon as I'd finished the food.

The front desk was deserted when I entered the motel, but I could hear loud mariachi music playing from a room behind the desk.

Probably passed out drunk, the son of a bitch.

After taking a surprisingly decent, cool shower, I lay on the bed, naked, letting the whisper of a breeze from the "chakka, chakka" fan cool me. The repetitious noise of the fan was actually soothing as

I allowed my mind to drift along for a few minutes before taking a review of the little knowledge I did have of El Salvador.

It is the most densely populated Central American country.

It is crossed by two volcanic mountain ranges, one being the Santa Madre Mountains.

It has a small coastline.

Their economy, much in decline since the early '60s, when the various drug cartels moved in and took over most of the private farms and ranches, forcing the occupants into poverty. The greedy, power-hungry cartels left most of the ranches vacant, allowing them to fall into disrepair and decay. The country, although under military rule and the influence of Fidel Castro, still relies on trade, manufacturing and agriculture, and now, of course–one of the reasons that I was here–the drug trade. Coffee, sugarcane, and cotton are still their major exports, trailing behind the drug trade.

To give the guy his due, ole Fidel actually does a great deal for his people, trying to bring about changes and improvements to the countries of Central America.

CHAPTER 7

Ricardo was waiting for me at the appointed time outside the motel. I had idled the morning away catching up on my sleep, had eaten breakfast at the little cantina, and had refocused my mind back to where it needed to be. The uneasiness about this whole thing returned, leaving a heavy knot sitting in the pit of my stomach.

Dark, ominous rain clouds were gathering, threatening to bring the day to a premature end, although the air still hung heavy and hot.

As Ricardo had promised, the ride into Santa Ana took about ten minutes. I had thrown the nylon bag containing my remaining American belongings onto the backseat as I entered the car.

Neither of us felt it necessary to talk during the drive, each of us caught up in our own thoughts. Once in Santa Ana, Ricardo easily maneuvered the car through the narrow streets, entering into the little plaza before taking a right turn down a side street. To me, it seemed that every street was identical to the next. The dreary, faded stucco walls were windowless, seeming to be endless and stretching the entire length of the street, with only the occasional doorway breaking the facade at different intervals. It reminded me of the alleyways back home.

The La Quinta Cantina was a much livelier establishment, with the sound of music, voices, and laughter spilling its way through the open double doors. This place also appeared to have more lighting from what I could see through the doors.

We were early, so I remained in the car for another ten minutes, watching the place where I was about to meet up with my asset.

An asset is the person in charge of the assignment.

All that I knew about him was that, like Ricardo, he was well connected in the area. Being a native of these parts, he knew the area and its people very well. He was the one who had made all the arrangements and details of the pickup.

The asset always had an assistant that worked for him, also a local to the area. His job basically was to watch our backs, to be the lookout and an extra pair of ears. He would observe and eliminate any potential threats to us.

Letting out a big sigh, I turned to Ricardo. As we shook hands, I said, "Thanks, man, it's been a pleasure."

"Good luck, John," was all he said.

As I climbed out of the car, my parting words to him were, "See you next time."

I never saw the troubled expression on his face as he drove away.

Taking a couple of deep, calming breaths, I crossed the narrow street. On the threshold of the cantina, I paused, long enough to do a quick survey of the room, before I casually walked to the bar.

I occupied one of the stools at the bar. The setup was the same as the little cantina in El Mora, only maybe twice the size. I could see that this was a slightly more upscale establishment as the tables had matching chairs. Christmas lights were strung haphazard along the walls. The bartender looked like he had actually made an effort with his appearance as he wore a real button-through shirt. I noticed that the cloth he was holding was marginally cleaner. I watched him swipe it around the inside of a glass; a filmy smear remained as he placed it back on the shelf behind him.

I hope they serve bottled beer.

CHAPTER 8

I was relieved when he popped the cap off a bottle of beer he pulled from a small fridge under the counter. Sitting at the bar, sipping on the beer, I took in the few patrons that were scattered around the room. Judging by their clothes, most of them looked to be farmers and field hands enjoying a cool beer after a hard, hot day's work. There was one table occupied by five loud Americans obviously enjoying multiple beers and their own jokes. They were most likely here on business and enjoying some R&R.

I watched as a short stocky man in his midfifties got up from a table in a corner of the room, approached the bar, and occupied the stool to my left. He asked for a beer before offering me a cigarette from an open pack he took from his shirt pocket. We were both wearing red shirts.

"Smoke, senor?"

"No. Thanks."

Picking up his beer, he nodded toward the table he had come from, saying, "Come, let us sit where we can relax and chat." *Enter my asset.*

Neither one of us sat with our backs to the room. He introduced himself, in heavily accented English, as Eduardo. "Call me Ed."

"I'm John."

"So everything is good so far?" he asked with a smile.

"Yes. Thanks."

Ed momentarily shifted his attention to a couple entering the cantina. The man was Caucasian, in his midthirties and wore a red tank top under a denim vest. The woman draped over his arm looked like a local floozy as she tottered alongside on ridiculously high lime-green platform sandals. Her V-neck shirt did nothing to hide the fact that she was extremely well endowed, the micromini skirt barely covering her ample behind. She could have been a beautiful woman if dressed differently. She obviously thought that she was hot enough the way she was.

Ed acknowledged the man with a nod as they made their way to the bar, where they occupied two stools. *Enter the assistant avec floozy.*

I wasn't surprised to see that the assistant was Caucasian as a few tourists often stay and settle down, after their vacation is over, to live and work here. God knows why.

Ed returned his attention back to me.

"So the details of the pickup are arranged. We go tomorrow, a place northeast of here. Any questions?"

"No." *This guy's big on details.*

Smiling, he said, "Good. Now we eat."

Later, he drove me back to my motel. His parting words were, "Ten a.m. I'll pick you up here." With that, he sped off in his dirty Toyota jeep, leaving me standing in a cloud of dust.

CHAPTER 9

True to his word, at 10:00 a.m. the following morning, Ed was waiting for me as I stepped out of the motel. With my Beretta in the waistband of my jeans, wallet in my pocket, it was with great trepidation that I climbed into the backseat of the dirty jeep. It was quite the classy ride, with tears in the canvas top and one door held closed with rope. The assistant was sitting in the passenger seat.

Once again nobody felt it necessary for conversation, leaving us to our own thoughts.

I was intensely focused, psyching myself up for the upcoming transaction.

My understanding was that Ed would do all the talking, which made total sense as my command of Spanish sucks.

We followed the same dirt road through green jungle, past green fields of various green crops, and into the mountains. The monotonous scenery once again not managing to hold my attention for long. I had no idea where we were or where we were going. Apparently, they didn't believe in road signs here. After what seemed like a decade, we took a turn onto another dusty dirt road. The constant flapping of the torn canvas roof and invasion of bugs was really beginning to grate on my nerves.

My immediate attention was captured as we slowed down and pulled up to a group of four to six rough, ruthless, mean-looking men. They were dressed in a mixture of jeans, dirty T-shirts, and drab green fatigues. Each one of them had an AK-47 trained on us.

Obviously rebels of some sort.

Killing the engine, Ed held his hand up to motion for us to stay put before climbing out and approached the men.

He spoke to them in Spanish for a few minutes before he returned to the jeep. One of the rebels climbed into the backseat beside me before we continued down the same road.

The knot in my stomach, growing larger as it roiled with emotion and turmoil. I felt trapped, with a sudden rising panic in my mind as I now realized that it was my door that was tied shut with rope.

At this point, I started to run different possible scenarios through my head. My training told me that this would be a perfect place for an ambush. This was definitely a setup. I was convinced that I was going to die.

The rebel was even pointing his AK-47 toward me rather that away from me.

They're going to shoot me execution-style and dump me out here where no one will ever find me. Feeling my Beretta pushing into me, I'm thinking that I should kill all three of them. I can only kill one, realistically, before I got killed. If I could kill all three of them, where would I go? I don't know where we are going, I don't know the area, I don't know what lies up the road ahead. I definitely don't want to go back down the road to face the other rebels. There's no way out.

I was sweating profusely, and it wasn't all from the humidity.

CHAPTER 10

I made the wise decision to ride this one out and see what would happen.

Shortly we pulled up to this old, dilapidated, what I assumed to be farmhouse.

There was heavy growth of vegetation that had begun to invade the exterior of the building.

On the porch, two more rebels were standing. This time though, their AKs were slung over their shoulders.

Good sign, right?

Once again Ed killed the engine, climbed out of the jeep, and approached the two men. I could feel sweat running down my spine like a trail of ants on a march.

Ed exchanged a few words with them before he disappeared into the building. After a few minutes, he reappeared on the porch and started to wave for us to come in. I was on high alert at this point.

All three of us followed Ed into the center of the main room. Directly in front of me were two old wooden chairs facing a battered desk. Sitting behind the desk was an important-looking man. He was in full fatigues; they were clean and sharp. He had that air of authority about him. I believe that he was in charge as when he spoke, the others stopped.

Off to the right of the desk, in an old, cracked, and worn brown leather armchair, sat another rebel.

Behind me sat another rebel, this time slouching on the matching worn brown leather couch. Sitting next to his feet was a large duffel bag.

I could tell by the quality of the old furniture that this was once a classy place.

Ed was doing all the talking with the guy behind the desk. After a few minutes, he turned to me, nodding toward the rebel on the couch.

Silent message–check out the bag for the money.

I walked over to the couch as the rebel unzipped the bag, revealing that it was indeed full of stacks of US paper currency. I looked up at Ed and nodded my head.

Silent message–it's good.

I started to relax some of the tension in my shoulders as everything seemed to be going well. Both Ed and the lead rebel were smiling and nodding their heads.

Suddenly, out of nowhere came a crack of gunfire, and I saw Ed's assistant drop to the floor, dead. Rapid-fire gunshots blasted through the air around me. I watched as Ed fell to the floor, dead. As the lead rebel rose out of his chair, drawing his pistol, he too was shot in the center of his forehead.

Reacting quickly, I dropped to my knees and threw the Beretta under the couch, and I placed my hands on my head.

CHAPTER 11

Everything now changed; the whole scene happened in slow motion, distorting and warping everything that I saw around me.

Within two very short minutes, everyone in the room was dead but me.

Everything was now silent. Nothing stirred; everything was still. The acrid smell of gun smoke drifting slowly through the air, mixing with the metallic smell of blood, began to fill my nostrils. The ringing in my ears from the gunshots left me feeling dazed and fuzzy headed. I was stunned and confused at what just happened.

As noises began to penetrate through to my conscious and my senses slowly returned, I had to think quickly before I started shouting.

I repeated over and over at the top of my voice, "I'm an American who's just here to buy drugs. I'm rich. I have money. This is my money. I just came to buy drugs."

I continued to shout as I was kneeling on the floor, facing the wall.

The new rebels were making such a commotion with their yelling and screaming at one another; of course I didn't understand what they were saying.

I continued to stare at the yellowing, moldy wall in front of me. A sense of both panic and sadness began to creep its way into my conscious as I suddenly started to think of my parents. Convinced that I was definitely going to die now, I wondered what kind of letter these sons of bitches would send to my parents. A lump came into my throat as I pictured my mother sitting weeping as she read the letter. Never knowing what I did. My whole life had been a lie. As a rash of emotions washed over me, I bit back the threat of tears. I was not afraid of death or of dying.

It's okay. Do what you're going to do to me. This is payback time. It's now my time to die.

Suddenly one of the new rebels hit me hard in the kidneys with the butt of his rifle. The force of it knocking me sprawling to the floor.

My face just happened to land in what was left of the face of the rebel that was sitting on the couch.

CHAPTER 12

An instant wave of nausea overcame me as I continued to lie there with my face buried in the still-warm, shattered, bloody remains of the skull. A gory mixture of gray brain matter, bloody tissue, and slivers of bone were smeared across my face. The scents of blood, shit, sweat, and urine were mixing together to make such a repulsive stench in my nostrils that I gagged. Trying to catch my breath, I breathed through my mouth.

I struggled to shut away the person in me and bring back the operative that I am.

Keep going, John, you ain't dead yet.

A frenzied assault began when one rebel kicked me hard in my side. I heard a rib snap. I groaned as a second and third kick followed. The third thudding into the small of my back, sending a withering shock of pain through my kidney and bowel.

Winded, I managed to pull myself to my hands and knees, sucking and gasping desperately for breath. Another kick to my gut caused my arms to give out, going straight down, and my chin struck the floor. My teeth snapped together.

I moved my tongue around the tacky, metal-tasting cavity of my mouth, checking for damage and broken teeth. I rolled onto my back. I tried to open my mouth to speak, blood bubbling from my lips. A mushy damaged sound was all that came out.

As I lay sprawled on my back, a rebel swung the butt of his AK, with as much force as he could muster, between my legs, smashing into my balls.

I couldn't scream. I couldn't find the air to scream. I twisted and jerked myself into the fetal position. A white knot of pain rose from my crotch and into my bowels and intestines, expanding into a withering sensation of nausea. My whole body tightened like a fist as I fought the urge to vomit. I was clawing at consciousness, fighting for each second of clarity.

The assault lasted for what felt like hours, when actually the brutality only lasted for about ten minutes before the lead rebel called a stop to it.

While I was lying there, remaining huddled in my fetal position, on the filthy, blood-spattered floor, more questions began to pass through my head.

Why aren't I dead?
Was I set up after all?
What had just happened and why?
Do they believe what I'm saying?

It was at this point that I made the decision to carry on this charade. I really needed to play up the role of the scared American spoiled brat on a drug-buying spree who obviously had more money than sense.

I had to try to convince them that my story really did match what I was saying. It helped that the duffel bag with US$300,000 was sitting next to me. If I convinced them that I was now an asset to them, they didn't need to kill me now.

As I continued to lie in the fetal position, drawing in ragged and uneven breaths, my arms were pulled behind me and were tied.

Every breath burning my lungs, one side of my chest hurting more than the other side where I knew and could feel that ribs had snapped.

An old, dirty, musty, foul-smelling hood was pulled over my head, the air getting hotter and heavier, almost suffocating me, diminishing my air supply, making it harder to breathe.

An arm under each of my armpits hauled me to my feet. Because they had just kicked the shit out of me, I was unable to bare my own weight, so they half dragged and half carried me outside. I knew we were outside as I felt the slight temperature change and the air stirring. I was then roughly thrown into the backseat of a vehicle. My two new friends joined me, one on either side. I could hear two other vehicles start up just before all four of our vehicle's doors were closed.

After a while of bumping and rattling around in the backseat, I lost track of the number of curves and bends in the road.

It was taking all my concentration and energy to breathe. My whole body was throbbing with the pain coursing through it.

I was angry at myself for allowing them to take me captive, my pride and ego bruised.

It was their game now. They were in charge, and I was just along for the ride.

CHAPTER 13

Not a word was spoken by anyone for the entire length of the ride. After a while, the vehicle took a sharp right before coming to an abrupt stop. We must have been at some sort of farm as I could hear the sounds of chickens crowing and goats bleating somewhere off in the near distance. The doors were opened as I was dragged from the vehicle. I managed to find my feet and stagger along with my two friends still gripping my upper arms. We got through two doorways before I was thrown down onto a dirty, dusty, musty-smelling wooden floor. Before leaving the room, they hog-tied my feet to my hands. The hood was still in place, and although it was half suffocating me, at least it kept the damn flies off my face. I rolled half on my side to help ease my breathing. Short, shallow breaths were all that I could manage. I remained still and quiet.

What's the purpose of what they're doing to me?

Do they want info about the agency?

Do they believe my story?

Do they even realize who I am?

Had they mistaken the assistant to be me?

They will *kill me at some point.*

Although the flies weren't able to play on my face, I could feel them crawling on other parts of my body where my clothing didn't cover my skin. The mosquitoes continued their feast on my already sore and sensitive arms. Lying there blind, my other senses had increased in their acuity. I used them to try to mentally collect information as I had been taught at the farm. I had heard one vehicle leave, so that meant that two vehicles remained. The door to the room remained open. From time to time I would hear footsteps come to the doorway, pausing briefly before going away again. Although the hood remained in place, I could sense that night had fallen. At some point, I heard the vehicle return, followed by a gaggle of giggling female voices.

A few minutes later, I heard footsteps as someone entered the room. I received a swift kick to the back, to rouse me, before being pulled up into a wooden straight-backed chair. The hood was removed, my eyes squinting, trying to adjust to the dim light. A couple of candles were the only light source, keeping some parts of the room in shadow.

The lead rebel (I call him chief) suddenly started this tirade and barrage of questions. He delivered his words quickly and in a manic staccato fashion, sounding like rapid gunfire. His arms were swinging wildly and gesticulating. He paced rapidly as he was screaming at me. Spittle dribbled down his chin, the veins standing out at his temples. His face flushed bright red as he repeatedly raged on.

"What are you doing here? You're spying on us. You want to take our money. You are trying to take over our operations here." Over and over and over again. He continued his paranoid rant for a long time.

Who is this crazy son of a bitch? Jesus, I'm captive to a fucking maniac!

I sat quietly and unmoving as I watched his performance.

I noticed that there were three women standing in the doorway, watching.

I knew that if I was to stand any chance of living, I had to personalize myself. I needed to make a connection with one of them.

One of the women appeared to be really uncomfortable with the scene. I could tell by her constant fidgeting, shifting her weight from one foot to the other, that she didn't want any part of this. She looked to be a little older than the other two, maybe in her midforties.

She made eye contact with me.

She was the one! I needed to connect with her.

At one point during a pause in his rant, I asked, "Can I please have a drink of water?"

The rebel that I had named Brutus, who was the one that I suspected was dealing out all my beatings, left the room momentarily, then returned with an old, dirty bucket in his hand, wearing his rotten-toothed grin on his face. He proceeded to throw the contents over me.

It was urine.

Holding back my revulsion, trying not to show any reaction, I let the urine run down my face. The chief laughed before asking, "Would you like some more, or have you had enough to drink?"

Smiling, I replied, "No. I'm fine for now, thank you."

This only irritated him, making him become more agitated as he continued his rant.

"Aww, American smart-ass, eh?" While he continued his temper tantrum and tirade of insults and repeated questions, I was receiving a barrage of backhand slaps and punches to the head and torso. I lost count of the times that I fell off the chair. I was so exhausted that I was unable to hold myself up. Finally, they got smart and tied me to the chair before resuming the beating and ranting.

They eventually tired themselves out, getting it out of their systems. They finally left the room, leaving me tied to the chair. My ears were ringing. My head felt dizzy and cloudy. I could feel that one of my ears was wet, probably bloody.

The woman walked up to me, took the front of my shirt, and wiped my face before leaving the room. I saw such compassion and sadness in her eyes.

As I sat there, I could hear the voices of the rebels and women talking and laughing. It sounded as if they were having themselves one good old time of it.

I hope they all get syphilis and die.

CHAPTER 14

I roused from the emotionally spent stupor I had drifted off to a noise that at first I couldn't make out just what it was. The icy hand of fear suddenly crawled slowly up my spine as I recognized what the noise was. With dread, I recognized the sound of glasses chinking together. They were drinking. My imagination came up with all manner of sick and twisted torture scenarios. They could probably really turn up the heat once full of alcohol. I suddenly felt very sick to my stomach. With my senses on high alert, I feigned sleep, just closing my eyes. Periodically, I would get slapped as one of them would check on me.

What seemed like hours later, the woman and a rebel came into the room. She was carrying a bowl and a spoon.

I hope that they're not going to now try to feed me shit, was my immediate thought.

To my relief, it was only rice and beans. After each mouthful, I thanked her. At one point, I asked her, "Why am I here? I'm just an Ameri–" I didn't get to finish my sentence as the rebel punched me in the side of my head. "Shut up. You no speak to her." With that said, they left the room.

It was a long and lonely night.

By dawn everyone was up and moving around. After about five times of me requesting to use the bathroom, two rebels came, untied my feet, dragged me to a hole in the floor, snatched down my pants, and plopped me over the hole.

I don't know about you, but I can't go with an audience. But I manage to overcome the prude in me and am finally able to relieve myself.

I was then hauled to my feet. My pants were yanked roughly back into place, and the hood was pulled over my head.

I was then dragged outside and thrown into yet another vehicle.

On the road again.

Jostling and bouncing around in the backseat with my two babysitters, we continued along what seemed like the same long stretch of road before I felt the vehicle slowing down. I assumed that we had reached an inhabited area. We took a few more turns before the vehicle slowed down and came to stop. One rebel got out. My ears were working overtime as I listened for any clues as to what was happening. The smell of gas drifted its way to my nostrils. Setting off again, I felt the vehicle speeding up as we obviously left the populated area. We rode for a while on a long stretch of road before the vehicle stopped, and I was dragged out of the vehicle and hauled to my feet, which they then untied.

"Walk," one of them barked.

This should be good. I'm blind and crippled. They are telling me to walk.

I didn't know where I was walking to, nor did I know what I was walking on. I walked a few steps before something caught my foot, tripping me, and I landed none too gracefully on my ass. Impatiently, they hauled me to my feet again and, with a swift kick in the back, sent me on my stumbling way again, only to fall down after two or three steps.

This is a joke. The dumb-asses can't possibly expect me to walk with a hood over my face.

After many more falls, someone finally got smart and pulled off the hood.

The brief and sudden rush of air felt good and cool on my face.

Panic leaped into my chest, and my bladder quivered as I saw that two of the rebels were holding machetes.

Oh my god, I'm dead now.

Definitely dead.

This is where they're going to kill me and leave my body to the jungle.

Oh my god, they're going to hack me up into little pieces.

Oh my god, I'm going to die now.

Oh my god.

CHAPTER 15

The two rebels brandishing the machetes, obviously getting a kick out of their intimidation of me, instead began to hack a rough path through the dense undergrowth. Now that the hood was off, the damn flies and insects returned to plague me. Ever tried to swat away flies with your hands tied behind your back? A rough path was hacked through the thick tangle of brush, vines, and trees as we moved along. I took a few steps and stopped and got pushed in the shoulder to keep me moving, took a few more steps, and stopped. This was the pattern for the duration of the very long day. I only opened my eyes long enough to see the path for about fifty yards ahead. The insects were really having a time of it now. I struggled to keep up with the rest of the pack as they were setting such a blistering pace despite walking on the roughly hewn path. It was like they were on a march through the woods on a well-worn path. They were oblivious to my difficulty to keep up. After a while, we stopped. Apparently, we were taking a time-out to rest and eat. I dropped to the ground where I was standing, totally spent and grateful for a halt in the marching. I was ignored while a meal was hastily prepared over a quickly assembled, crude campfire before being devoured. My mouth was salivating, my stomach growling its protest at not being fed.

Looking over to where they all sat, eating, laughing, and drinking, I thought to myself, *You fuckers all look alike. I'll bet that the same gene pool is swimming around in each of your bodies. You look like a bunch of inbreeds with your long stringy hair and ratty beards. I'll bet that the total IQ for all of you cocksuckers isn't above thirty.*

I watched as the woman with the kind eyes went around each rebel, scraping any leftover scraps from their plates onto one plate, before coming over to me with the same plate. I was temporarily grossed out–some of them weren't in the habit of practicing good hygiene–but I quickly got over it as it was food, and I must have food to survive. After she fed me, I again thanked her.

We quickly resume to trekking our way through the jungle, the endless jungle. The sky blocked out by the webbed green canopy overhead, a solid and continuous wall of greenery, more greenery, and then more greenery.

We came upon a stream that was pretty rugged and rocky, but there were places that it pooled and looked to be about a foot deep. I spied my chance. As I was teeter-tottering my way across, I faked a stumble and fell into the stream, rolling around like a turtle on its back. This proved to be highly amusing to everyone. They were all shrieking with laughter, slapping their thighs, and pointing at me. As I was rolling around trying to wash some of the crap off me, I thought, *The dumb jackasses don't realize that I'm doing this on purpose. What a bunch of dumb fucks. Go on, keep on laughing, I'd drown you sons of bitches any other time.*

Enjoying the brief coolness that the water was bringing, I sucked up as much as I could before one of the rebels hauled me to my feet again.

We ended up trekking until dusk. Apparently, we would be camping out overnight. As the primitive camp was being set up, two rebels cut down a sapling and stripped it of its branches. They then hog-tied me again and slid the sapling through my hands and feet, wedging each end of the sapling into the crook of a branch of a tree.

Black edges began to swirl around as the excruciating pain wracking my body threatened to plunge me into the depths of unconsciousness. I was sure that my shoulders had dislocated as they were suddenly forced to support my entire body weight. This position made it near impossible to breathe. It was restricting my chest so bad that I was only able to take the shallowest of breaths. The blood rushed to my head as it hung down, making it feel like it was going to burst. I could feel every vein standing out, ready to pop. The roaring of the blood as it rushed to my head was deafening.

As the rest of the camp settled down for the night, I was left hanging three feet off the ground, trussed like a hog ready to roast.

It took me a few hours before I managed to work my body so that I was half lying with my shoulders on the top of the sapling. At least I was able to breathe a little easier. I took a few more breaths before I finally allowed myself to succumb to the black edges of unconsciousness.

CHAPTER 16

Spending the whole night hanging by my feet and hands had really done a number on my already battered and broken body. I wanted to scream out at the sheer agony that was ripping through my entire body as they took me down. I had gone numb overnight, my body trying to slowly wake itself up. My hands were so swollen they felt like they were going to burst, still tied behind my back. I wriggled them to try to get the circulation going again. I was forced to take short panting breaths at the tingling and jolts of electricity running through my arms and shoulders as the feeling began its slow, painful return. A cold sweat enveloped my entire body, bringing nausea to the pit of my empty stomach, bile rising up into my mouth, threatening to spill out for everyone to see.

I'll be damned if I puke and give the sons of bitches the satisfaction of seeing my pain.

I overheard the rebels talking to the kind woman with the compassionate eyes. They were calling her Maria.

After she had fed me my scraps, I pleaded and told her that I would surely die if they kept hanging me up every night. I was unable to breathe properly. If I died, then they wouldn't get their money.

Maria promised me that she would try to talk to them.

As they were breaking down the camp, I noticed her talking with the chief, looking over my way as she spoke. Her face held a scowl as she talked rapid, and her hands did a lot of gesticulating. They went back and forth in Spanish for a few minutes. The conversation sounded heated, their voices getting harsher, their hand movements wilder. He dismissed her with a sudden wave of his hand as he laughed and walked away, shaking his head.

It was apparent that the trek was to continue through the jungle for another day.

As I was stumbling along on rubbery legs, trying to block out the discomfort and pain that was shrieking at me, I came to the realization that in order to survive this ordeal and as a measure of self-preservation, I was going to have to disassociate myself. I was going to have to take myself off to a better place in my head.

I tried to keep track of the days, distracting myself by making up rhymes in my head.

Today is day 2. If they ask again, I'll say, "Fuck you." This is day 2.

Again the flies and insects continued their relentless mission to eat me alive. Insects were constantly crawling in my eyes. Blinking my eyelids did not dissuade them any. They invaded my nostrils and the corners of my mouth. I tried not to open my mouth; otherwise, in they would go. The tight bindings on my wrists were beginning to chafe and cut into my flesh, causing abrasions. This only gave the flies something else to feed and crawl on. The mosquitoes continued their assault on any skin that wasn't covered by a piece of clothing. As I trudged along, tripping over roots and vines, stumbling, trying not to fall, I began to relive the series of events that had led me to be here.

My thoughts turned to the first time that I had met Marylyn.

Between assignments, it wasn't unusual for me to do some surveillance work in Canada. A lot of anti-US factions entered the United States through Canada. The surveillance work was Monday through Friday. I would leave out of Hanscom Air Force Base, a small base in Bedford, Massachusetts. It was an agency plane that would fly me into Ottawa. From there we then flew on to Toronto and then Vancouver.

It was early on in my agency days, in 1974. I met her when I was taking my first flight to Toronto. I was told that there was a stewardess on the flight who would pass on the info of the surveillance job that I was going to do.

I had asked if she knew me—yes.

"How will I know her?"

"She'll do you a favor."

The flight was to be a short flight of just over an hour.

As I was pushing my carry-on bag into one of the overhead bins in coach class, this drop-dead-gorgeous stewardess said that there had been a cancellation in first class and asked if I would like to follow her. Dumbfounded, I just stared at her. "Follow me," she said as she took my bag and carried it to first class. It was while she carried my bag that she, unbeknownst to me, secreted an envelope inside.

We chatted easily back and forth during the flight. She told me that she was a courier for the agency. She mostly flew on the international flights with Air Canada to Europe.

As I was deboarding the plane, she put a hand on my shoulder and asked if I had everything that I needed. I replied that I probably didn't.

Marylyn was a beauty; she was tall, slender without being skinny, had curves in all the right places and luscious long dark hair. She had a bubbly personality and was well put together, immaculate in her way of dress.

It wasn't until I went to the men's room at Toronto airport that I discovered the envelope.

When we eventually stopped for the day, it was dusk.

While camp was being set up, to my horror and disappointment, I saw the rebels once again cut and strip a sapling before making their way over to me.

Obviously, Maria's little talk had not helped.

I prepared myself mentally for yet another extremely long night filled with excruciating pain along with plenty of discomfort.

Dear God, please send me the strength to endure another night trussed up.

CHAPTER 17

At dawn the next morning, they took me down and threw me on the floor. I didn't even move. I lay as still as I could. The world was ebbing and flowing around me in waves as I struggled to hold on. A part of me wanted to go under, to escape the pain, turn down the volume on my screaming ruined body. I was already drifting away from myself, the hurt being balanced out by a growing dreamy sensation of floating.

Maria came to tend to me, and I once again pleaded with Maria for her to persuade them to not truss me up. I had already started to die.

That morning, we once again began to march through the deep, dense jungle. My body was in really bad shape. My thoughts remained clouded, my movements slower and stiffer. I found myself stumbling and falling more often. The messages that my brain was sending out weren't too clear, causing me to become increasingly more uncoordinated.

I let my thoughts drift into my safe place. I found myself thinking of Marylyn.

Our meetings were infrequent. Marylyn passed information on to me probably only six or seven times. Each time that our paths crossed, we would talk and get to know a little bit more about each other. Personal information was never divulged. It was agency policy to not get involved with fellow agents or operatives.

Marylyn was really just a courier; she didn't normally do field assignments or any covert operations.

This one particular assignment of mine, a surveillance assignment, called for a young couple under the ruse of a week camping in the north woods of Vancouver. Marylyn was asked along.

We met up in Toronto and were to meet up with two other agents in Vancouver before we drove into the woods.

Marylyn and I spent two to three days shopping for the supplies that we would need for our camping trip. We practiced being a young couple, feeling more at ease with each other as time went on. We developed this easy banter between us. We held hands.

Marylyn was a city girl and didn't like the idea of spending a week in the great outdoors.

"Ever been in the woods before?"

"No. I tend to avoid it. I like the city. Will we be staying in cabins and motels?"

"No, Marylyn, we'll be sleeping under the stars in sleeping bags, roughing it, you know?"

"Sleeping bags? On the ground? I don't know about this. What I consider 'roughing it' is a two-star motel with no room service."

Oh boy! Was she in for a surprise!

It took her four hours to pick out a pair of hiking boots! They were brown, they were not fashionable, they weren't comfortable or stylish, they didn't match her clothes, they were heavy and ugly and clumpy.

Marylyn was not too impressed at having to wear a camo jacket either. Wait until she found out that there were no toilet or shower facilities.

When we were packing our backpacks, I told her to pack just the essentials to try to keep the packs light. Our meanings of 'essentials' didn't quite match. It was a very disgruntled Marylyn that boarded the plane for Vancouver.

Before we arrived at the baggage claim area, we were met by a guy in a shit-brown suit. He was midforties, tanned, lined face, greased-back dark hair with hints of gray beginning to show. I instantly disliked him. He had an air of arrogance about him that oozed out of his every pore. He started up with lewd comments directed toward Marylyn. Really derogatory smart-ass remarks and innuendos. "Did you get to fuck her yet? Nice rack. I'd like to get between those thighs."

He disgusted me. Abruptly cutting him short, I said, "Let's just keep it business, shall we?"

We headed down to the baggage claim area where his partner was already unloading our luggage. We all caught a cab to a hotel. The two jackasses shared a room, as did Marylyn and I.

We were to do surveillance on this Iranian businessman who was supposedly going camping in Vancouver. It was suspected that he was going to meet up with someone during his trip. Our job was to watch and photograph the meeting.

Marylyn threw a fit when she found out that it would be ten days and not seven in the woods.

"Ten days, you told me a week. I don't have enough clothes or makeup for that long. My nails need a manicure before then." On and on she went.

"You don't need to wear all that stuff on your face. You look just fine without it."

"What do you know about it?" She was fuming.

It didn't help when she took out her Smith and Wesson revolver. It had pink handgrips.

"Hardly camouflaged, is it?"

Her sassy reply, "It's not like I'm going to wear it on my waist now, am I?"

Grudgingly I left my memories as I let reality creep into my conscious again. It was once again dusk, now at the end of day 3, as I lay watching the process of the camp being set up for the night. Things were beginning to fall into a kind of routine. There was a familiarity about each day.

After Maria had finished feeding me, the same two ugly-ass rebels walked over to where I was slumped. Dreading their next moves, it took me by surprise as one of them cut my hands free. I saw that they were varying shades of black and purple and extremely swollen to the point of bursting. I didn't really feel them at this point. I tried not to feel anything.

I attempted to move my fingers to get the circulation going again. As I was doing so, my wrists were retied in front of me with smaller rope. I could feel the beginnings of sensation slowly prickling and tingling its way back into my hands.

CHAPTER 18

My shoulders slowly started to scream out in pain at finally being back in their proper place. I'm not so sure that I felt better at this point. The pain had woken up and was a throb running through my entire body. My hands both repulsed and scared me at the same time. They were so grotesque they could hardly be recognized as my hands. I stood staring at them as I experimented with wiggling my fingers, all my attention taken up with getting the circulation to return.

Brutus shoved me forcefully in the chest. I lost my balance and ended up on my ass as I cracked the back of my head against a tree. Stars danced before my eyes, and I winced at the sudden impact of body against solid, ungiving object. The rebels then proceeded to lash me tightly around my chest to the tree. Although this was a more favorable position than being trussed up, I still had trouble breathing, but I was so thankful at the change in position. I might even be able to get some sleep.

I later realized that I was once again at the bottom of the food chain in this hellhole of a jungle. There happened to be millions of huge black ants crawling along their paths up and down my tree. I was an obstacle put in their way, and they must, of course, climb all over me before continuing on their way. They just added to my collection of insects that I had accumulated along this wondrous of journeys through the jungle.

I just hope the bastards don't start to bite me!

I must have dozed off as I woke to a sudden jolting pain in my right leg. Someone or something was kicking my right foot, hard. I looked up to see the leering grin of Brutus and a couple of his buddies.

They were standing over me, casually smoking their shit-stinking cigarettes, talking and laughing as they kept glancing down at me.

Oh god, what are they about to do to me?

I soon found out as they each in turn slowly ground out their cigarettes on my shoulders. I braced myself, anticipating the coming pain, only it didn't come. The cigarette hissed and sizzled and smoked before going out. The rebels were shrieking with laughter, falling over themselves, patting one another on the back and totally enjoying the whole spectacle.

You dumb motherfuckers. I realized that it is my sweat-soaked shirt that is extinguishing their cigarettes and not my skin. What a bunch of fucking retards you are.

Thank you, God! Thank you.

It looked convincing enough to them, the lingering smell of singed fabric, the hissing of fire meeting what they thought was my flesh, all added to their sick amusement. They left me alone after they had all ground out their butts on me. I was relieved that, for once, their torturous game had misfired on them. For once, the laugh was on me.

They sat rehashing it with the other rebels as they sat around the campfire, laughing and slapping one another on their backs.

Small things amuse such small minds.

Well, they couldn't help it. None of them had ever had the chance to be formerly educated.

They were recruited at a young age and only know what they have been shown.

They are taken from their simple poverty-stricken families who can barely feed them. They are a nobody, just like everyone else in their community, and adopted into the sick and twisted world of the rebels. Here, they are fed, clothed, given attention, and accepted as a "soldier" of the drug lords. They are taught to be brutal, uncaring, and ruthless. They live like kings in their eyes, being treated better than they have ever known. They are taught to torture and kill and to enjoy it. They glean a tremendous sense of power from inflicting pain and suffering to others, enjoying it, getting immense pleasure and satisfaction from it all. They are made to feel like someone, someone who is important.

Even the wearing of military uniforms feeds into their sense of being a soldier, of being self-important, of belonging. They are kind of brainwashed into believing in the cause, each one of them as dumb and stupid as the next.

What does that make? A bunch of idiots who are as dumb as a bag of hammers.

It is only the human race that is cruel to their own kind. It is only the human race that does it for the sheer thrill and enjoyment of doing it. They know no different or no better.

They live like a bunch of wild animals, not bathing, never changing their clothes. They have this big aversion to personal hygiene and grooming. It's almost primitive the way they live. Everything is done in excess–drinking, eating, partying, torturing.

I am so much better than these stinking animals. For a brief while, I actually allow myself the little luxury of feeling good about myself. It breathes a little life into me again. I regard myself as being a lot farther up the food chain than them.

CHAPTER 19

As the jungle woke up to a new day, its sounds began to penetrate my conscious. I became aware of all the different varieties of birds singing their dawn choruses. With those sounds, as they gradually became louder, came the conflicting emotions that washed over me with each new dawn. For a few seconds, I would feel relief that I had made it through yet one more night. Hot on its tail followed a roiling knot of dread in my stomach. Now I had to survive through another day. Would it be the same as yesterday, or would it be worse?

It could always be worse.

Before each day began, it was always already down the shitter!

Today is day 4. Hope you all catch something from the whores!
Today being day 4.

The two younger women certainly provided a wide variety of entertainment for the loser rebels. Their voices and frivolity could be heard well into the night, every night.

I knew this as I would only be able to snatch very short naps. The rebel pulling watch would check on me with annoying frequency, kicking or slapping me awake each time he did his rounds.

Although sleep deprived, I was mentally clearer headed and not as stiff now that they had lashed me to the tree for the night. I really hoped that this would continue and become a pattern.

This time, as we set off once again to hack and thrash through the jungle, I was attached to a rebel by a rope tied around my wrists, like a dog leash, and dragged along.

Taking a couple of careful breaths and exhaling slowly, I prepared myself for the day ahead. I was determined that I was done being afraid of these dumb motherfuckers and followed along on the rough path, trying to look more confident than I felt.

The previous night's self-pep-talk had helped to revive me a little. I'd be damned if I showed these assholes my fear or pain.

The monotonous rhythm of being dragged along through the green dimness of jungle soon had my thoughts wandering off to different places.

I found myself back in Vancouver with Marylyn.

We set off early the next morning in a rented station wagon with woody walls.

It was fall, and there had already been snow in the high country. I could see it dribbling along the dark peaks, slightly coating the forest. The morning was bright and clear, with the hills sporting colors so bold it almost hurt my eyes. The colors–the golds and russets, the scarlets and bronzes–just exploding with fall.

Looking out the window–Marylyn and I had opted to take the rear seat–we were mesmerized by the scenery. We stared out at the vast, glorious, yet terrifying space, the way the forest crept up the foothills as we headed north.

"I need to buy a rifle and a hunting license. Stop at the next hardware outdoor store we come to."

"Why do you need to buy a rifle? We have one already," asked the jackass driving.

Not wanting to alarm Marylyn, I swallowed my first response. Because we're deep in bear country. A pistol won't kill a grizzly. Instead, I said, "Who the hell do you know who goes on a hunting trip with a pistol?" You fucking asshole! Duh!

After about an hour, we came upon this little inhabited area with a sundry of small buildings. One of which was a log cabin that obviously catered to campers, hikers, and tourists. Its sign boasted "fresh bait, milk, and your last chance to buy ammunition."

"We'll stop here. I'm going to check out their hunting section."

I perused the vendor's selection of rifles, which I was pleasantly surprised to find was pretty large. I chose a Remington 308, with manufacturer-mounted scope bench sighted in for about twenty yards. I also bought topographical maps of the area.

Over a light lunch, we discussed our plan of action. I told the two jackasses that I needed to resight my rifle, but I needed an open area to do it. When they started to complain, I told them that they could stay here in town while Marylyn and I went. Studying the map, I found an area that had been logged and that looked like it had been abandoned for a while.

Marylyn and I spent a pleasant afternoon sighting in the Remington, shooting it so as to get used to how it fired. Anywhere away from the two morons was great. They didn't speak much. When they did, it was either sexual innuendos or in a condescending manner. They thought they were better than us, the arrogant pricks.

CHAPTER 20

The road that we were on was the main road leading through the forests of British Columbia. Along this road were these little scenic outlooks where tourists could park and view the scenery. As we approached such an outlook, we noticed that the two Iranian men had parked and were still sitting in the car, obviously waiting. We pulled into the same outlook past their car, stopped, parked, and got out. We were pretending to do the tourist thing and pointed out things of interest to one another, all the while keeping an eye on the Iranians still sitting in their car. We had to wait around to see who they were going to meet. Eventually, a jeep pulled in behind their car and stopped. A few minutes later, both cars pulled back onto the road at the same time. Game on.

We followed them, at a distance, for about an hour before they pulled into this gas station with a motel-and-souvenir-store combo attached to it. The two cars both pulled up to the same pump, one on each side. We had pulled up in front of the store to sit and watch. We made out that we were studying the map.

The Iranians and the two new men struck up some sort of conversation. They paid for their gas, pulled up to the motel, and entered. A few minutes passed before all four of them walked out, and all left together in the Jeep Cherokee.

The Iranians looked like tourists as they were clean-cut, in casual shirts and slacks. They looked like businessmen on a break. The other two dressed in camouflage shirts and slacks looked to be more at home in their surroundings. In fact, they were pretty skuzzy looking. They really looked like a couple of hobos that had already been in the woods for a month.

We followed behind while taking photos and notes and watching carefully. They didn't seem to be doing much hunting or walking, just spending a great deal of their time in vehicles.

We lost sight of them, so we stopped, parked, and studied the maps. I noticed that there was a hiking trail that we could climb up, which would eventually bring us out on a small precipice where we would be looking down onto the road. This would hopefully give us the advantage of being ahead of the men again.

We decided to hike the trail. We packed our various supplies into day packs along with our weapons.

I found myself grinning as I watched Marylyn struggling to pull out her pack from the station wagon. I knew it would be heavy. Marylyn didn't know the meaning of 'packing lightly.' I stood there watching as she wriggled into the shoulder straps.

"So much for chivalry," she muttered to herself.

"Hey, I heard that. Want me to carry your water bottle?" I couldn't help myself.

"No, thanks, I'll manage, smart-ass."

We kept up a brisk pace as we ascended the trail. Again no one spoke much. We were too busy trying to keep our breath. The two assholes led the way. They were anxious to find the men and looked like two excited schoolkids on a day trip to the forest. A couple of times I had to tell them to keep the noise level down. I wondered how much field experience these two idiots had. They sure weren't acting like they had any, to my eyes.

We must have walked for about two hours. All the time, I was bringing up the rear with Marylyn in front of me.

Though Marylyn looked out of place in her hiking boots, I could see that she was determined to keep up and make it look easy.

Did she realize how out of her element she looked? As I looked at her, I saw that her dark jeans and boots looked to be fresh out of their packets. Even her figure-hugging, long-sleeved camouflage shirt looked like something out of a boutique by the way she was wearing it. She looked like a model posing as a camper.

Once we had reached the precipice, we hunkered down and waited.

CHAPTER 21

And we waited.

We had stayed just inside the tree line in an attempt at not being seen.

While we were waiting, the two jackasses were pacing up and down, trying to spot the jeep, impatient at the delay as time went on. Again I had to remind them to keep the noise down and to stay out of sight. I was confident that we were now ahead of them somehow.

I took advantage of this downtime to refuel my body by taking a snack and a drink. Reaching for my canteen, I unscrewed the top.

"Great weather for a hike."

Marylyn scowled as she looked at my canteen. "Don't you have a cup?"

"Packed with the china, ma'am," I said as I continued to drink.

"Then I'll wait."

"Suit yourself." I shrugged as I finished my drink and replaced the cap as I turned away from her. I could feel her eyes burning a hole in the back of my head. I knew that her water bottle was empty. I wouldn't let her go thirsty. I would fill it for her at the next stream.

We had waited probably a good two hours before the Jeep Cherokee came into sight along the road below. Lucky for us, they happened to pull into the scenic outlook below.

They stopped. It was difficult to get a clear view of them through the trees. The two jackasses were getting more impatient and agitated by the minute. They couldn't get a clear view of the men. They couldn't take photos as we were too far away. They needed to see what was going on. They were constantly moving around to try to get a better view of the men, whom I had not yet seen exit the jeep. It didn't help that it was quickly approaching dusk, their daylight threatening to run out on them.

"We need to get closer. We can't see properly. We need to go down there. We are running out of time. It'll be too dark to see soon." There was a hint of panic and urgency in their voices, the desperation showing in their movements as they hurriedly began to gather up their belongings.

"Hold on there, wait a minute. Just stop a minute. Something doesn't feel right."

We went back and forth for a few minutes, debating whether or not we should get closer.

Finally I said, "You can go down there, but I'm staying here. There's something wrong with the picture. I'm not entirely comfortable with this."

Marylyn stood like a deer caught in the headlights, her eyes wide as the conversation began to heat up. "I'm going to stay with John."

"Yeah, yeah. You stay here with pussy boy while we go and get the job done." Their arrogance showing through as they purposefully put a swagger in their step.

We turned on the walkie-talkies that we had bought.

"Better turn that thing down. The squelch of it will give you away."

"we know what we're doing, John boy." Whatever, ass-wipes.

They consulted the map before they set off. They were going to sweep around and approach the jeep from the rear, which was about a three-quarter-mile hike. You could hear them tramping through the woods as they left, stealth not being one of their stronger skills, damned idiots!

Marylyn and I watched their movements through binoculars as they worked their way down the steep terrain. I kept training my binoculars on the parked jeep. There was still no movement. My feeling of unease only increased with every passing minute. Something was wrong here, my gut kept telling me.

I kept watching as the two jackasses made their approach from the rear of the jeep.

I was startled at the sudden sound of what seemed to be automatic gunfire that exploded and echoed through the trees. I didn't see where it came from, but I did see the two jackasses go down. I knew they were dead. I got the familiar fluttery feeling of fight or flight in my gut.

I heard Marylyn's sudden sharp gasp of breath as she watched and realized what had just happened below. I dug a hole with my boot and placed the walkie-talkie in it, scraping the earth back over it with my boot.

"We have to go. We can't go back to the car, we have to leave our stuff back there."

Marylyn just nodded her head in stunned silence, all the color drained from her face. The fear apparent in her wide-open eyes.

"It looks like we'll be spending a few days out in the woods. Maybe four to five days. We have some supplies and maps. We walk at night, take it slow."

With my pack on my back, I started walking, leaving her no choice but to follow.

CHAPTER 22

As we made our way quietly and cautiously through the forest, the night had moved in on us. We needed to stop for the night and get ourselves together.

"We need to take up in a tree," I told Marylyn. A puzzled look passed across her face, asking the silent question why.

"If we sleep on the ground, we'll be found." I left out the bit about bears and other creatures finding us.

I found a tree that was suitable. Using some of the rope that we purchased for the trip, I hauled our packs up into the tree and secured them. Then I began to push Marylyn up another tree, following close behind. Once we had ourselves situated, I used another piece of rope to secure ourselves to the tree.

"Why are you tying us to the tree?"

"If we fall asleep, we'll more than likely fall out of the tree."

Being a city girl, all this was new territory for Marylyn. I could see her mind working overtime. I also knew that being in a dangerous situation was foreign to her. The fear remained in her eyes, but I could see her fighting to keep a tight leash on her emotions, not wanting to seem weak and helpless and vulnerable.

"So what do we do now?" she whispered.

"Sit and wait. See what they do." I was holding the now-loaded Remington across my thighs.

"How do you know which way to go and how to get there?" Good question.

"I've got a compass, and I know how to use it, if that makes you feel any better."

"Hmm." My lighthearted attempt at reassuring her went unappreciated.

The only reason that I knew I had fallen asleep was because a noise brought me back awake. As I sat listening, I realized that it was no animal that I could hear shuffling along the forest floor. Gently placing my hand over Marylyn's mouth, I signaled for her to be quiet and to listen. I walked my fingers in the air to indicate humans walking below.

Although the night air was cool, a thin sheen of sweat had broken out over my entire body. My adrenaline was pumping through my veins, causing my senses to be on high alert. I did my best to push the fear that I was feeling out of my conscious. I worked hard at not letting it show. Marylyn didn't need any encouragement to be afraid.

The four men from the jeep came within about three hundred yards of our tree as they moved through the dark forest. I could hear their muffled voices as they moved down the ravine and kept walking. All the time, Marylyn's hand had an iron grip on my sleeve, that wide-eyed look on her face. I covered her hand with mine and nodded my head in an attempt to reassure her that we were okay.

I made us wait for at least another hour. I wanted to be sure that the men were not in the immediate vicinity when we descended the tree.

I reluctantly dragged myself back to the present as I realized that night was fast approaching, that we were going to stop and make camp for the night. There was definitely a pattern evolving as we made our way through the jungle. I had absolutely no idea where we were or where we were heading. For all I knew, we were just going in circles in the same area around and around. It all looked the same to me. It was one huge wall of green.

As I watched Maria collecting the scraps to make up my meal, I once again let myself feel the hatred that I harbored for these animals bubble and churn in my gut, threatening to spew out and make me do something stupid.

Reeling in my emotions, I told myself that I had to maintain. I was not going to let these bastards get the better of me. As I stood there, still tethered to my keeper Brutus, I looked at him and thought, *If you went to school for twenty years and then graduate, you'd only progress to being a moron then! Jesus, you stink! You never wash or change clothes. You sweat excessively all of the time, you are lower than a pig.*

It slowly dawned on me as I was standing insulting him that I stunk just as bad as he did. It was quite a sobering thought, and I was disgusted at myself that I had become like them. I was constantly covered in a slimy sheen of sweat, and I attracted flies and insects like a piece of roadkill lying on the side of the road. I'd given up trying to swat them away; it took far too much energy to do so. I was so exhausted that I was relieved as they lashed me to a tree.

I dared not think about what I was eating as Maria spooned it into my mouth. If I let myself think about it, I could easily gross myself out enough to make me throw it back up. Seeing as they only saw fit to feed me once a day, I'd rather hang on to the scraps that I was fed to nourish my depleted body. As each day passed, I could feel my body being slowly depleted. The sores around my wrists were worsening; green pus now oozed from them. My head had a relentless pounding in it that just wouldn't quit. I just wanted to be left alone and to be able to close my eyes. If I could do that for long enough, maybe it would subside a little.

Once again, as this too was so obviously becoming a nightly ritual, Brutus and his pals came over to play. They were smoking their cigarettes again, and I knew the game they were about to play. Tonight I was ready for them. I started to squirm away from them, cowering and whimpering as they once again found great pleasure in inflicting pain upon my body.

I was silently laughing at them. They still didn't realize that my shirt was the only thing being harmed. I offered them my back as a target so that they wouldn't use my face. I found it hard to believe the full extent of the thrill that they achieved from burning me. They truly were a bunch of sick and twisted fucks.

As I sat there in the dark, ever watchful, I discovered that I could use my long hair as a curtain over my eyes so that I could keep them closed. When I heard the guard getting close, I just had to move my head a little, and he would be fooled into thinking that I was awake. That way, he would just walk past me without stopping to give me a rousing slap or kick. I could at least rest my eyes.

CHAPTER 23

Day 5 began to show itself slowly. Sunlight trying its hardest to penetrate through the thick green canopy of foliage. Most of the time, it was pretty gloomy in the jungle as the foliage was incredibly dense. At least then the sun wasn't beating down on my uncovered head unmercifully. Everyone else had the luxury of wearing a hat, not me. Sometimes we would come across an area that was open to the sky, allowing the heat to shimmer off the top of my head. The headache was continuous now. I knew that it was the combination of dehydration, heat, and sleep deprivation that attributed to it. I could find no relief. The heat gripped me with its sweaty hands, squeezing and wringing the energy right out of me like water from a rag.

When we came across any kind of stream, I would throw myself down into it, drinking greedily as much as I could before Brutus would drag me away. Maria always managed to reason with them to allow me to drink again, so I would guzzle down as much as I could, only to have my body make me throw it right back up again. As I would lie there puking my guts up, Brutus would fill his canteen from the stream while fixing his eyes on me and grinning that god-awful broken-toothed grin of his. I was really growing to hate it. He would then take a long, hard, guzzling drink, allowing the water to overspill down his chin and onto his chest. As I watched him drinking, my dry and blistered mouth and throat would start to work, in anticipation of slaking my endless thirst. He really enjoyed taunting me. It took all that I had to not react to him, telling myself to look him in the eyes and show my defiance and arrogance. I really had to dig deep at times like these. I wanted to gouge out his eyes and stuff them down his throat. The inbred son of a bitch.

Back on the farm during training, we were told that there is always a way out of every situation, always a way out.

Oh yeah? The magic fairy going to come and untie my hands after giving me an infusion of energy?

As we would make our way through the jungle, along the hacked path, there was always something trying to grab a hold of me, tearing at my clothes and exposed skin. Branches would slap me in the face and body. Thorns would rip at my flesh, adding to the gradual degeneration of my skin. Half of the time, I was numb and didn't feel it. Like the bugs, you just got so used to it you no longer let it bother you. I would be concentrating on just putting one foot in front of the other, taking a breath, and then another.

Step, step, breathe, step, step, breathe, step, step, breathe.

Chanting it in my head to myself over and over again, hundreds and hundreds of times each day.

Today is day 5. I'm still alive, I think. Today is day 5, step, step, breathe. I'm still alive, step, step, breathe. Step, step, breathe.

CHAPTER 24

Step, step, breathe. Reminding myself to open my eyes a few seconds, just enough to be able to see maybe the next fifty yards, making sure nothing would tangle with my shuffling feet and put me on my ass. Step, step, breathe, step, step, breathe. The monotonous chant was in a way soothing and helped to calm the constant anger I felt. I'm certain that Brutus purposefully let branches smack me full in the face. The sting and lingering tingle would momentarily bring me to the present before I would slip back again into my chant.

It felt like we walked, or in my case, shuffled, hundreds of miles a day. I don't know how far we did actually walk each day, but it felt endless. Not knowing our destination made it feel even worse. From sunup until sundown, we were on the move, the rebels obviously in much better condition than me, the city boy. They tolerated the smothering heat and pesky bugs. They were as sure-footed as mountain goats, never seeming to stumble or lose their balance, unlike myself who was stumbling all over the place. When I wasn't stumbling, I'd be staggering and shuffling. With all the beating and abuse to my body, the exhaustion had a negative effect on my overall coordination, making it difficult to walk. I just wasn't able to. It felt like I was walking in three feet of snow. Lifting my feet up and down took so much energy to do, energy that I just didn't have.

I felt a million years old, aged well before my time both physically and mentally.

For some unknown reason, I suddenly began to think back to the first lie that I ever told.

This coming from someone who has made a living and skill out of telling lies shouldn't make me feel as guilty as I was feeling now.

I was about seven years old, and I was out with the neighborhood kids just messing around. It was early spring, so it was also still cold out. The snow was beginning to melt, causing these small streams to run down to the lake that we lived on and through the woods. I was the youngest, weakest, and smallest of the group. I was often teased and bullied because of my size. I was puny for my age, looking a lot younger than my seven years.

Alan Hitchcock was a year younger than me, yet he was twice my size. He wasn't allowed to do much like other kids as his mother was very overbearing. They weren't an athletic family, but by god, could he throw rocks. I can remember that he could knock a squirrel out of a tree by throwing a rock at it. What an arm he had. He could've made it big as a pitcher in baseball, but he was quiet, not adventurous, and wasn't the brightest crayon in the box.

Now Tina Ritari, she was my age, but a tomboy. She was small but stocky and came from a Finnish family. She was good at floating paper cups down the little streams. She always won the races.

Bob Joyal was also my age, yet twice my size. He was French Canadian. We would hang out all the time together all through our young childhood. None of us came from rich families. We had no toys and had to make up our own games to occupy ourselves.

The other kids had no problem jumping and leaping across these streams, one after another, as we raced through the woods. My size made it difficult for me to make it all the way over this particular stream. I leaped and landed smack in the middle of the icy, cold water, on my ass. All the others were laughing and making fun of me sitting there with this wide-eyed look of shock and surprise on my face. It took a couple of seconds to realize just how cold the water was. My delayed reaction just adding to the good ass-soaking that I had received. On my way home, I was dreading telling my mother how I had gotten so wet. I knew how mad she would get as I wasn't allowed to play like that. I had scarlet fever as a kid, and my health suffered for years after. I was kind of delicate, my mother only looking out for me by endorsing such rules. Shit, I'd probably be in bed sick with a bad cold the next day. So I decided not to tell her the truth.

Instead, I told her that I was sitting on a wet log by the stream, watching my friends jump over it. She just looked at me, saying, "Run along and get out of those wet clothes."

As I raced up to my room, it dawned on me that she had not questioned my explanation. I'd gotten away with the lie. I had just told my mother a lie

and *gotten away with it! Doing a little victory dance in my room, I jumped up in the air and punched the air with my fist and whooped in glee.*
I'd been lying ever since, honing it into a great skill.

I must have been smiling at the memory as the next thing I knew was I felt my leash being forcefully tugged, making me stumble and fall to one knee. My knee just happened to land on a rock. I gasped as the white-hot pain shot through my leg and into my stomach, making me feel sick and dizzy. Brutus just stood there laughing at me.

My anger seethed despite my exhaustion. He pulled me to my feet by tugging again on my leash. The dizziness in my head cleared, but the sickness lingered a while. It was very painful to put weight on that knee, and we only probably had another two million miles to walk.

The fucking cocksucker. I'll kick you in your balls with my good leg. Just you wait, buddy! Then, while you're down, I'll kick you in the head, making sure I get your face. Hey, it'll probably improve it! You can't get any uglier!

CHAPTER 25

Somehow day 5 to day 7 managed to merge all into one. The scenery unchanging, becoming very monotonous. I slid into automatic pilot mode to try to preserve my energy while I visited other places in my mind. I found that I was disassociating myself more and more as an attempt to escape the reality of my situation. I was trying to shut down certain areas in my brain.

I opened my eyes in the dawn light of the dense jungle. Thoughts began to seep into my conscious.

I got to thinking about Marylyn and what I'd done when I went off the reservation. I really was okay with it. I'd do it again; it was well worthwhile. It was a self-gratifying thing to do for myself. I knew it wouldn't change anything or bring her back, but I'd done what I wanted to do. I was at peace with myself over that. No regrets.

In this world, you can do anything that you want to do. Anything. *But you have to be willing to pay the consequences. I felt that I was paying right now. I knew that my thinking was distorted, driven by my emotions—anger and hate. Yet I felt that I had still evened the score.*

Day 7, this is hell, nowhere near heaven. Day 7.

Sometime in the afternoon, we came upon what looked to be like some sort of settlement. We were on a rise so could see down onto it. There was a cluster of dilapidated-looking shelters that only had three walls so couldn't really be classed as buildings. They looked like something a farmer would build for his livestock to shelter them from the elements.

Two military-looking jeeps were visible, parked outside one of the shelters.

We were signaled to sit and stay while two rebels were sent ahead to scope the place out.

We waited until dusk before we made our way down to the settlement.

The chief was talking to who looked to be their leader. There were maybe fifteen to twenty of them. They too wore fatigues but appeared to be more put together than the band of vagabonds I was traveling with.

I was immediately taken before their leader and pushed to the ground.

In his heavily accented voice, he barked, "Who ees these peece of chit?"

As I opened my mouth to explain my story, I received a swift boot to the head and told to shut up. Lying there in the dirt, I thought that I was suddenly in a huge bell tower with a lot of bells pealing in my ears.

The world was ebbing and flowing in and out of darkness as two men dragged me along the floor by my leash. My face scraped along the rough and uneven dirt ground, my shoulders screaming their protest as the rest of my body dragged behind.

When I came to a stop, I was under one of the shelters. I was sat in and tied to a wooden chair. As I realized what was about to happen, again the memories of previous interrogations came back with adrenaline-enforced clarity.

The beating began with the heel of a boot connecting with my chin, chattering my teeth together, the sheer force of it snapping back my head before my chin slowly rolled back to rest on my chest. The darkness kept on coming in waves; everything slowed to slow-motion speed, struggling to hold on to consciousness. A part of me wanted to go under, to give in and let go to escape the pain.

The questions continued. I didn't try to answer; I knew it was no use.

I sat staring at their leader standing in front of me. Mocking and making fun of me in front of everyone else, laughing in my face. Puffing his chest and feathers out to make himself look even bigger and more menacing, trying his hardest to intimidate me.

Another ruthless bastard. Another Billy fucking Badass strutting his stuff in front of his men.

I stared at his body through distorted eyes, which were making him waver and ripple as I fight for each second of clarity.

"We got yo munny, we no need yo now."

"I can get you more. I can get you a lot more." I was hoping that my mouth was working right and that they could understand what I hoped were words falling out of my bloody mouth.

"We got yo munny, we gonna kill yo now," the leader excitedly screamed. I was having difficulty understanding him as even his voice was slowed and slurred. He sounded like a bear growling while chewing a mouthful of toffee.

Again I slurred, "I can get you more money."

Brutal impulses sated, they left the room. Two guards were left to watch me slobber and drool down my chest. The world was spinning madly as I shivered against the sickness and pain throbbing through my entire body. Thankfully, I was left tied to the chair. I tried to stop the spinning feeling by stamping my feet on the ground, much like when the bed spins with a bad hangover. The guards were highly amused at this. The world continued to come at me in waves, their faces all distorted as if they were in the house of mirrors. I fought the unmerciful nausea swimming and swirling in my stomach. It took a great effort to not throw up.

After a long time had passed–I knew this by the way the guards were fidgeting, and I could see their discomfort at having to stand there all that time–the chief and Billy Badass returned.

His eyes were hard and staring as he walked toward me. I braced myself in anticipation of being struck. He looked at me for a few seconds before hawking up a globule of phlegm and spit it into my face. Satisfied, he nodded as he turned and left the room.

Fuck-face, you disgusting pig. I want to make you eat my foot as it kicks out all of your teeth. You sanctimonious little prick. I hate you and all of your little inbreed lackeys.

To my horror, we actually spent the night in this hellhole.

CHAPTER 26

Remaining in the chair, I was at least able to rest my body a little. My mind stayed alert throughout the night. I didn't feel comfortable knowing that Billy Badass and the gang were around. They were likely to slit my throat in the wee hours.

I was actually relieved when we once again headed out on our endless trek through the jungle.

When will this end? Will we ever reach our destination? Are they just going to drag me around until I drop dead? What the fuck, man.

My sheer delight at leaving those fiends behind was enough to keep me going through another day in the jungle.

My thoughts returned to those woods in Vancouver . . .

After about an hour of waiting to make sure that the men were out of the area, Marylyn whispered that she had to pee.

"Pee down the tree, like I just did."

"Eew, I can't, plus I have to do number 2."

So we climbed down the tree, and while she was taking care of her business, I retrieved our packs from the other tree. There were coyote tracks and bear tracks around the base of the tree!

I informed Marylyn that we needed to vacate the area now.

"Can we use a flashlight? It's awfully dark." I could hear the fear in her voice.

"No, hon, it'll make a big target out of us. We have two choices as I see it. We either go the way they came, or we can follow them. But we absolutely must keep them in our sights at all times."

I consulted the map as I was unable to decide which way to go. I looked to see if there was any other way that we could get to civilization without being detected by the four men. There was a small village about fifteen miles away. If we took it slow and cautious, we could make it in three to four days.

"We are almost out of supplies, how are we going to manage?"

"Good point, we have no choice. They are not leaving here until they find and kill us. I don't see any other way."

We followed the same routine, keeping away from people, keeping to the densest parts of the woods, climbing trees at night.

On the third night, as we settled ourselves in our tree for the night, Marylyn pointed at a faint light in the distance. "What's that?"

It looked like a small campfire. "Let's go take a look."

We walked to a small ridge in the woods where we could see down onto the small campfire. Still at a safe distance, we watched through our binoculars. As I was watching, I made out one of the Iranians' faces in the glow from the fire.

"It's them. I can only see three. They must have one doing lookout."

My mind began to run a couple of possibilities through it. I talked out loud as I was thinking.

"It's our advantage, they've not seen us, so they have no idea how many of us there are. We don't know if they are actually coming for us or trying to get out of here. We don't know them or their capabilities, but they can definitely kill us. We are still two days' hike from the village. I think that I can take a shot at one of them."

"Are you crazy?" Marylyn asked incredulously.

"Maybe, but I need to get to a good position where I can take a shot at them. There was a rocky outcrop back about an hour ago. We flee to there after the shot and hunker down."

It took me a couple of minutes to find a tree close enough that would afford me a good vantage point. I climbed the tree that was within three hundred yards of the camp. It was a cold, clear night with a sliver of a moon to guide us just as it could spotlight us for the predators that were stalking us, but too many trees were in my line of vision. I had left Marylyn waiting at the base of the tree. I was sure that she was trembling in her little boots, her imagination doing overtime. Every shadow was a potential enemy, every rustle in the woods a warning.

Just as I was about to abandon for a better tree, the man doing lookout came into my field of vision and stood in front of the fire, giving me his back and a perfect silhouette of him.

With tape that I carried in my ditty bag of sniper supplies, I had taped the muzzle of the rifle earlier to act as a flash suppressor.

Steadying my breathing, I took aim and sent the shot. I watched through my scope as the man fell on top of the fire before rolling into one of the other men. They immediately started to scurry and scatter, like roaches when light is shone on them.

I quickly descended the tree, and the two of us made our hasty retreat to the rocky outcrop. Once there, we wriggled our way between boulders, preparing to sit and wait.

I told Marylyn to get comfortable as we would stay here all day until dusk.

Now the hunters had become the hunted. They would be more wary now, not going to pursue us as quickly. They would be more hesitant.

We dozed off and on throughout the day. I'm sure that Marylyn was really glad for the rest. I know that her feet and legs must have been hurting.

As dusk arrived, I was certain that they were going to take off now that they were a man down. I didn't feel that they were still pursuing us.

We started to make our way to the village, which was only a half day away, but I took us the long way around, taking it slow and being cautious, stretching it out to a day and a half. All our supplies had gone, so we were forced to drink from streams to satisfy our thirst.

Marylyn never once complained. I knew that she was afraid and very tired. I admired her for her bravery; not once did she whine.

CHAPTER 27

Days 8 and 9 blended into themselves as I gladly settled into the familiar routine once again.

By way of a dirt road, we began to see signs of civilization. There were some horse farms, and in the distance, the village was visible.

We waved down this old truck that was puttering its way toward the village. The farmer driving it was a French Canadian, and Marylyn, thankfully, put her French to good use.

We were by this time all scratched up and dirty from our days in the woods. We probably didn't smell too good either.

In French, she explained that her stupid boyfriend had gotten us lost. "Is there somewhere we can clean up and call friends to come pick us up?"

We hopped into the bed of the truck as we were taken the rest of the way into town. There were a few small buildings, including a gas station and post office.

My senses were being at their acutest. I entered the convenience store connected to the gas station. The attendant spoke English, so I explained that we were lost and had been wandering for days. "Could I please use the phone to call for a ride?"

I dialed the 800 number. "We have been lost in the woods, got separated from our party. It looks grim as there is only Marylyn and I. Everything has gone south, which is where I would like to be heading. We need to be picked up."

Meanwhile, Marylyn had been talking with the farmer about a place to stay. He mentioned a hotel a few miles out of town. She convinced him to help us get a room at the rooming house next to the store. That way, our friends would be sure to find us.

The rooming house was a quaint three-story building. We got a room at the front but had to share a bathroom with the other guests on our floor.

Once in the room, we dropped our packs and took off our boots.

Marylyn stood there, physically and mentally exhausted, as quiet tears slid down her pale cheeks. A wild mix of emotions washed over me as I just took her into my arms. She fell against me as she sighed heavily and let go.

As we stood in the embrace, something changed between us. Both of us were wrought with emotions. We looked at each other at the same time, our faces only inches apart. Our lips connected in a deep kiss. The kiss intensified, neither one of us pulling away but pushing into it. When we did pull away, our breathing was ragged. Our eyes mirrored each other's need.

"Just stand there," I said, touching only mouth to mouth as I unbuttoned my shirt.

"Let me taste you a while. Here." My lips cruised along her jaw. "Here." Up to her ear. "You can trust me."

"Uh, uh." She let out on a sigh.

I tossed my shirt to the floor. "Let me look at you, Marylyn." Slowly I slid her shirt from her shoulders, let it fall to the floor. She was long and slim, subtle curves and strong angles, her skin glowing. "You're beautiful."

I cupped a hand to the back of her neck, drawing her slowly toward me. My fingers combed through her hair, experimenting with its weight, lifting it, letting it fall while my mouth rubbed over hers. I sampled the exposed line of her throat, nibbled where her pulse throbbed. I skimmed my hand down to her breast. A moan escaped her lips as she shivered with pleasure, her body quivering at my touch. My hand slid lower over her hip, across her stomach, brushing then pulling away.

Her eyes were huge, focused on mine. Her hands gripped my shoulders for balance before her fingers dug in as I continued to stroke her flesh.

I knew that she didn't expect my tenderness. She was expecting it to be a fast groping, grappling match with my grunts and groans as I took her.

"John?"

"Hmm?"

"I can't stand up anymore."

CHAPTER 28

I lifted her into my arms and laid her gently on the bed.

"You still have your pants on."

I covered her, letting her grow accustomed to my weight.

"It's best that they stay on a while."

I trailed a line of kisses down her throat, and with a shudder running through me, I took her breast in my mouth. She arched, her breath hissing through her lips. Her hips began to grind along with mine. Her hands were fisted in my hair, urging me to feed.

I heard her gasp and sigh and whimper. Her response to every touch was as free and open as any man could only hope for.

I took her mouth again. I needed it like I needed air. Our tongues danced in a tango.

I stroked my hand up her long length of leg, stopping just short of her center. Her breath was coming quickly now, fast and shallow, as her nails dug into me. I brushed her, lightly, found her hot, wet. My fingers stroked her, and everything happened at once. Her body went taut, bucked, shuddered, and then went slack again. A small cry escaping her mouth.

I rolled off her, leaving her lying in the tangled covers.

CHAPTER 29

As I unsnapped my jeans with shaking hands, I prayed that I wouldn't fumble now. My blood was pounding through my body, throbbing loudly in my head, my groin screaming.

Tossing aside my jeans, I remembered what I always carried in my wallet.

I had to get my nerves under control.

Nerves fluttered in my stomach as I placed myself over her. Her arms coming around me as I slid into her. It took every ounce of control to stop myself from plunging mindlessly into her. Willing myself to go slowly, I placed my hands on each side of her head.

I watched her face as dark pleasure flickered across it. She matched me stroke for glorious stroke, a small smile pulling at her mouth. I finally emptied myself into her with my face buried in her hair.

Our orgasms had left us happy and totally spent.

With all the fear and horror of the past few days, we had managed to find an oasis. For tonight, and only for tonight, there were only us in this room together. Tomorrow would come soon enough.

Afterward, we lay next to each other dozing, just basking in the peace and safety of our room, our bodies still quivering and slick with sweat.

I heard Marylyn gather some things and leave the room. Most likely heading to the bathroom.

She stepped back into the room, rousing me from a pleasant after-sex doze.

She wore a flimsy peach silk robe trimmed with ivory lace. It stopped midthigh, the belt cinched tight to accentuate her narrow waist and full breasts.

"You did know that we were going camping? I told you to only pack the bare essentials."

"I did. Lingerie and makeup happen to be essential to me. Besides, a woman has to be prepared for any occasion!" was her sassy response.

With that, she unscrewed the top of a jar of expensive-looking crème and began to smooth it onto her long legs. I knew that she would smell of jasmine when she was done.

After a long sigh, she said, "You know that this won't ever happen again." She said it as a statement rather than in a question.

Letting out a big sigh of my own, I said, "Yes. I know," smiling at her.

The next morning, as we were sitting having coffee in our room, two black jeeps with tinted windows pulled up to the front of the rooming house.

"That's them," I said in relief. We picked up our belongings and went out to meet the man who had just stepped out of one of the jeeps. He was wearing khaki pants, polo shirt, and aviator sunglasses and a warm smile on his face.

As we were crossing the street toward him, I said, "We're looking to head south."

"I'll just bet the hell you are," he said with a Texas drawl as he opened the back door to one of the jeeps.

CHAPTER 30

Day 10 began just like the previous days and followed the same monotonous routine.

Once again, as night began its descent, we came upon the outskirts of what looked to be an actual village. It had a semblance of civility about it. I could see a lone power pole. There were about twenty wires jerry-rigged to it and sprouting out like tentacles to the various buildings. My god, we were getting closer to civilization!

While we were waiting for night to fall, I noticed there were some signs of life within the filthy little village. I could see and hear chickens and goats milling around, getting ready to settle down for the night. Also, a couple of mangy-looking cats and dogs were scavenging around in the filth and trash-filled sewage ditches. The village had the general appearance of being old, tired, overused, and extremely worn out. This was a very poor area. The buildings were very dilapidated and in poor condition, some barely able to support themselves. Even from where we waited, you could smell the putrid and rank aroma of their outdoor sewage system, drifting along on the evening air.

At nightfall, we made our way toward the village. Everything was quiet. One of the dogs set up barking, sounding the alarm. I believe that the village already knew that we were coming. The air seemed to get somewhat heavier and damper. It felt like it was somehow trying to steal my breath, suffocating me with its unnatural heat.

Outside one of the falling-down buildings, I was caught unawares as one of the rebels suddenly grabbed me around the neck, putting this ridiculously big dirty, rusty knife to my throat. Instantly, Maria was at my side. "Don't do or say anything, or he kill you."

I didn't need telling twice. Brutus was still holding on to the other end of my tether, standing nonchalantly as if nothing was wrong.

I felt a quick icy trickle of fear run down my spine, carrying a quick surge of panic with it.

As quick as it started, it ended, and we were making our way into the building.

Fear walked with me as we stepped into the main room, a sense of déjà vu flashing through my mind as I recognized the beat-up old wooden chairs and scarred table, which seemed to be identical to the ones that had occupied every other building that we had been in.

This time, it wasn't the rebel I'd named as Brutus who dealt out my beating but the skinny slimy one with snake eyes who had pulled the knife on me. Standing there with my hands still tied in front of me, I could do nothing to avoid the sharp, short-armed, bare-knuckle punch to my face. He leaped as he slammed his fists into my face, letting out a triumphant scream as he spun snake fast to land a kick into my shoulder. I dropped helplessly to my knees, wheezing in an agonizing breath, concentrating on the source of pain as it spread from my shoulder, down my arm, and across my chest. He continued to throw punches at my face and throat, alternating with rabbit jabs to my ribs. My burning throat and lungs fought to draw in air, my vision blurring and doubling at the vicious pain screaming through my body. Throbbing, making me burn, inside my head, I screamed. I had no breath to make a sound, no strength to even crawl or writhe at the hideous pain he was causing me. I dropped helplessly to the floor. I could hear their voices, but they were smothered by a drowning fog of pain. I sensed that he wanted to pound me to pulp, a mad and murderous look in his eyes.

The chief indicated for him to stop, two other rebels having to pull him away and out of the room.

Lying there on the floor, my whole body was screaming at the pain that was fierce and full.

Had he killed me? If so, I wish to God death would get a damn move on so the pain would stop.

CHAPTER 31

I managed to somehow pull myself into a sitting position, my head spinning in revolutions.

"*Jesus H. Christ, Mary, and Joseph.*"

I sat with my head balanced on my up-drawn knees, my arms hugging my knees in an attempt at stability as the world continued to spin around me. This apparently was the signal for the chief to start on one of his tirades. Taking his cue, off he set in one of his maniacal screaming tantrums. Face beet red, veins popping out at his temples, erratic pacing across the floor in front of me.

Through the fogginess, I fought to comprehend what he was asking me. He had his face inches from mine, his spittle showering me as he screamed out his questions.

"Who you call? Who you call? Who you call?" over and over. I saw his eyes bulging with the strain as he fired the questions rapidly.

He reminded me of a machine gun, *Ratatatat, ratatatat, ratatatat.*

"I have a number to call," I managed to croak out.

"I have a number to call. I have a number to call to get the money," I repeated myself, trying to break through his screaming.

My god, he's lost it, he's nuts, totally out of control. Please, God, help me here!

He stopped midrant. His eyes had that wild crazy look to them; he was breathing heavy.

Quietly, I confirmed, "I have the number to call to get the money."

He motioned for one of the rebels to untie my hands. I was hauled to my feet and shoved down a hallway to the next room. Hanging from the center of the ceiling was a single sizzling lightbulb. Its flickering glow lighting only the immediate area beneath it, keeping most of the room in shadows.

They are going to juice me.

The thought quickly jolted through my dull senses, then I saw something that brought a glimmer of hope to me. I saw a black beat-up rotary phone sitting proudly on a table all by itself. "Here I am." I could almost hear it shouting to me.

I got shoved into the table, stumbled, unable to keep my balance. Both myself and the phone fell to the floor.

"You call now," ordered the chief in a quieter, somewhat calmer tone.

Easier said than done. I had to try to get my fingers to work and my brain to recall the secure line number to the agency.

Struggling to insert my index finger in each hole of the rotary dial, I dialed the number.

Only I dialed the wrong fucking number!

CHAPTER 32

Fuck me. Now I'm done for!

As I was once again on the receiving end of a blow to my head, I thought, *I've really fucked up now.*

The chief impatiently thrust the phone receiver back into my hands and motioned for me to dial again.

"Look, my hands, they don't work. Let Maria dial the number for me. Please," I pleaded.

I held the receiver to my ear with my right hand while my left hand was held on a small table with a knife resting against my wrist.

Maria dialed the number as I gave it to her.

It rang and rang and rang for what seemed like forever before it was finally picked up. I immediately started talking.

"Hey, Uncle John, this is John." There was the briefest of pauses, but it was long enough for me to realize that the person on the other end was surprised to hear my voice. Now I was convinced that I had been set up and should be dead by now.

"Johnny, my boy, I've been worried about you. Where have you been?"

"I need your help. I've been taken by some men. I told them that you had money that you would give them to get me out of this nice place."

There was a long pause. I knew that there were a number of people listening in on the conversation. I asked the chief, "How much?"

"One million US," was his swift reply. My heart sank. I knew that was an unreasonable amount to ask.

"Did you hear that, Uncle John?"

"Yes, I don't have it."

I relayed the message to the chief. He was most displeased at this and screamed at me, "You fock! You tell me he has munny, you lie to me."

With that, he snatched up the phone from my hand and screamed into it, three hundred thousand dollars, we call again tomorrow!" and broke the connection.

I was then dragged back to the main room and thrown on the floor. My hands were retied in front of me again.

Later, Maria came in to feed me.

"I don't know if he can come up with the money," I confided in her.

"He not let you make too many more calls."

"I know. I'm sorry. Thank you, Maria."

As I lay on the floor, a mix of emotions ebbed and flowed over me as my anger gave way to the pain.

CHAPTER 33

I was surprised the next morning when it became obvious that we were not staying but going on the move again through the jungle. Like little robots, we followed along the path leading through the dense green jungle.

It was during this time that I allowed sad memories to invade my thoughts.

Myself and another agent, Driesdale, whom I worked with a great deal, were in France. We had just completed an assignment and were waiting to come back to the States. We were in the little town of Le Bourget, north of Paris. We had rooms in a small hotel in the 60 Avenue de la Division Leclerc. The hotel was the Bar de L'hotel de Ville. It sat on the corner of two converging little streets, which made the building a wedge shape. The ground floor was occupied by a small café and bar, the other two floors occupied by rooms and bathrooms.

One morning a note was slid under the door of our room.

It was from another agent who wanted to meet us in the café downstairs with some news. This wasn't the usual way that we communicated between each other, so Driesdale and I were very wary, yet curiosity compelled us to go.

We found the agent waiting for us at a small table in the back of the café, out of the way of the traffic passing through the café. It was very busy, so we tended to blend in nicely and go pretty much unnoticed.

The news he gave us floored me.

Marylyn had been killed.

My mind wouldn't compute the information that I was hearing. A jumbled mixture of thoughts and emotions began to run through my head all at the same time, making it hard for me to concentrate on the details.

Apparently, she was in Prague, Czechoslovakia, on an assignment with another agent. She was doing her usual kind of assignment, exchanging information, when it happened.

The agent working with her escorted her to this luxury apartment building, a known and much-used "safe house," leaving while the exchange would take place, coming back some time later to meet up with her. Only she wasn't waiting for him, so he went to the apartment and found her dead. It was looking like it was an assassination by a well-known international assassin. He had a particular, gruesome signature m.o. (modus operandi) or calling card.

The agency believed it to be the work of an East German by the name of Grueber, a particularly sadistic bastard who did fee-for-hire killing for anyone who had the money.

I had so many questions swirling around in my head I couldn't think clearly.

I was stunned, angry, sad, devastated, my body trying to shut down to escape all the thoughts reeling through my head.

"I have to see her."

"No, you don't."

"Yes, I have to see her. I want to pay my last respects. I won't rest until I've actually seen with my own eyes that she's really dead." Desperation clung to my voice.

"I'm telling you, man, you don't want to see her. You've got to just let it go, believe me on this."

"He tortured her, didn't he?"

The agent just nodded his head somberly, stating that he had no more details. I suspected he knew everything and was just withholding the gory details to spare me. I could tell by Driesdale's silence that he too felt the grief that had its tight grip on me.

CHAPTER 34

The agent did finally tell us where in Prague her body was being held.

Obviously, it was all hush-hush, and the cleanup crew had gone in and taken care of everything, leaving no evidence behind. The agency wanted no one to know that anything had occurred.

Driesdale and I found the small private, nondenominational chapel where Marylyn was being held. Because of the delicacy and secrecy of the situation, the agency couldn't very well use the local morgues and funeral directors. This chapel was a known safe house, tucked away on a little side street. It did hold services for the few people who frequented it. Downstairs in the basement was where the secret work of the undertakers took place.

The agents of the cleanup team were abrasive in their manner toward us; we didn't belong there. But they did fill in more details as to what occurred. They were terse, but respectful, appreciating our grief over a fellow agent.

According to the intel that they had, the motivation behind the death was not robbery or a foreign agent trying to obtain information. The exchange had evidently taken place as the envelope that Marylyn had was replaced by a new one, and it was still with her when she was found. All her jewelry and her purse were left untouched.

She was found by the agent who was on the assignment with her. He had apparently left her at the building for six hours before returning. It didn't make any sense; none of it did.

Why was Marylyn targeted? She was pretty low on the totem pole of agents; she only did courier work, just passing on and receiving envelopes of information. She was a genuine stewardess for Air Canada. Admittedly, she was an easy target, and she was very vulnerable, but still, why her?

It was felt that it was the work of Grueber because of him leaving his mark on her. It was thought that it was a senseless vindictive act by a small power-hungry cell of individuals who just wanted to fuck with the USA and the CIA because they could. It was as if they were sending the message that they could get to our agents.

After much persistence on my part, the cleanup team finally, yet reluctantly, allowed us to view her body. Knowing that it had been the work of Grueber, I knew that this was going to be bad, really bad.

CHAPTER 35

It was horrific. The sheet was lifted to show us a body that had been unmercifully tortured. I fought back the nausea as I stood looking at what was once a young, vibrant, and very beautiful woman. The body that lay before us was difficult to identify both as a person or woman. We simultaneously gasped in horror as we took in the details.

The multiple mass of black and purple bruises covered her entire body, telling us that she had taken a brutal beating.

Two of her teeth had crudely been pulled out with a pair of pliers.

Three of her well-manicured fingernails had been ripped from her right hand.

Three severed fingers from her left hand, initially thought to be missing, had been found stuffed down her throat.

She had been repeatedly and brutally sodomized with a broom handle, which Grueber had broken off while it was still in her rectum.

Both of her nipples had been hacked off and had been stuffed up her nose.

The medical personnel informed us that all this had been done prior to her death.

I was unable to control my gagging any longer. I'd seen enough. A fresh wave of sorrow mixed with my anger as I fled the room. As I leaned over dry retching, all I could see in my mind was Grueber's mark.

He had taken the green scapular that I had given to her a little while after the Vancouver assignment and driven it into her forehead with a six-inch metal spike. My breathing came in short panting breaths as I fought to regain control. This made it more personal.

CHAPTER 36

All that I was able to see was red in my enraged state. I let my anger consume me and bubble up and flow over, spewing out with it all the emotions I had so far held back.

The problem was that I had allowed myself to get close to her. Something that we were aggressively encouraged to avoid.

Her body was to be cremated to cover up the torture and her whereabouts at the time of her death. Her family would receive her ashes along with a confabulated story of her death. It would probably be caused by a gruesome car accident, with false newspaper articles appearing in the local papers. My heart ached for her family. What a cold and harsh way to hear of their loved one's death.

As my grief overspilled, tears silently running down my cheeks, I said, "I will find and kill the bastard that did this to her. I will track and hunt him down like the animal that he is. I won't stop until I find and kill him. She didn't deserve to die this way. The pussy picked an easy target, the wrong target."

Driesdale stood beside me with his hand on my shoulder, trying to calm me down.

"I loved her too. I loved her like a sister."

"I've got to take some time off, take a vacation, anything. I'm going after him. I've had enough of this, they're just going to lie and cover everything up in a letter to her family. It's not right, not fair. She didn't deserve this to happen."

"I know, I know, you need to try to calm down. You can't go thinking like that."

"I don't give a fuck anymore, I've got to do something."

"You need to leave it be, let it go. It's none of your business," one of the cleanup agents tried to reason with me.

"The hell it isn't!" I was now in full rage mode.

"It was not your assignment. You are not a member of that team. You need to go home."

"No way, I'm going after him."

"You need to go home," the agent repeated himself as he dismissed me.

I turned to Driesdale. "I don't expect you to come along. I'll do it alone. But I need to take some time off."

"Don't do this. It'll be the beginning of the end."

"Maybe it will, maybe it's time."

Driesdale tried his hardest to dissuade me, but I was adamant. I had a new mission.

The agent tried one last time. "You can't do this, you know it's against protocol."

"Just tell Uncle John that I'm taking a vacation."

Resignedly he sighed. "I'll tell him," he said as he walked away.

Driesdale turned to me, smiled, and said, "You can't do this without me. You can't even find your way out of the bus terminal."

I smiled as I knew that he was right. He was the linguist of the team, and without him, I'd be useless.

I was physically and emotionally spent and allowed him to lead me back to our hotel.

CHAPTER 37

I realized, with dismay, that no phone calls would be made today. We had moved away from the small village and what little bit of civilization there was. It was looking less likely that I would get out of this alive. My body was in really rough shape; bruises and abrasions covered my entire body. Hell, I had bruises over bruises over bruises. I had taken so many beatings I'd lost count. My body was so broken and so worn down. I was numb; everything was past feeling. I'd remained on automatic pilot, just plodding along, following Brutus and his gang. I was just going through the motions now. One foot in front of the other. One breath after another.

I found myself trying to convince myself that I had to go on, I had to continue. I could not let these imbeciles win. If I gave up now, they would have won, wouldn't they?

In training, we were told that if we kept our heads, didn't allow our emotions to take over, to think it through, we would make it.

I remembered the session in training at the farm when we role-played being taken captive. The instructors didn't seem to be role-playing. They were serious about it and didn't seem to be acting at all. They hooked us up to a hundred-volt battery to see how long we lasted before we started to show signs of breaking down mentally.

We were continually shocked until we gave out. We pissed and shit ourselves, our muscles jumping and twitching, losing control with the electrical pulses passing through our bodies. Most trainees lasted about three days. I made it just over four days. One trainee at one time actually lasted for over five days.

What exactly is it that keeps us going? Isn't it amazing how much punishment the body can stand? We are so much stronger than we realize. Half the time, we don't even use 50 percent of our total potential. Our everyday lives don't require us to push ourselves beyond the boundaries of our comfort zones. We may experience a hint of it when traumatic things happen, like life events such as the death of a loved one, suddenly being struck by poverty, or disabled by an illness or accident. Even then, we really don't dig deep into our reserve. We never really get tested and pushed so hard that we have to resort to survival mode.

I knew that I was now in survival mode, and my brain had taken over from my conscious thinking as at every stream or body of water that we came across, I would throw myself into it and drink in the water that I so desperately needed. I was so dehydrated. My head was pounding worse now than when I was being kicked in the head. My body felt numb. Nothing hurt anymore. It was gone beyond hurting now. My senses had gone. My thinking blurred, not being able to think straight. Sometimes not even able to make a thought. I was zoning myself out from the world.

I was in a good place before I drank the water as I couldn't feel anything or think coherently, then I would drink. I learned not to guzzle great amounts down at one time as my stomach would just reject it, and I would spend precious energy on throwing up. Instead, I would take small quick drinks, taking my time resting in between, allowing my body to get used to it and to accept it.

It was then, as my body recovered a little, that I would once again be hurled back into that dark, bad place where I could feel all the pain and misery again, all the flies and mosquitoes crawling and biting and feeding on me. I could think more clearly as I returned to reality. Every time, my very first rational thought would be, *You stupid dumb fuck. You don't learn. You keep bringing yourself back. You keep doing this to yourself. Who's the dumb-ass now?*

CHAPTER 38

A fresh wave of sorrow joined the jumbled mix of emotions already swimming around in my mind. It was now day 12, and my hopes were diminishing rapidly. I didn't have any strength left to keep fighting this. Mentally I was breaking down. I no longer saw any options for escape. I knew that even if, by a miracle, I did get loose, I wouldn't have a clue as to where I was or to where I would go. I had resigned myself to the fact that here in this jungle I was going to die. I wished they would just kill me and be done with it. The relentless mental and physical torture had done its job. I had finally come up against the edge of emotional exhaustion. I once again allowed the person inside me to creep in and take over. I found myself thinking about what my parents were possibly doing right now as I, unbeknownst to them, sat here in this hellhole, waiting to die.

I was having myself a really good pity party and wanted to be left alone with it.

I remembered back to when I had given the green scapular to Marylyn.

We shared the Roman Catholic faith. The green scapular is a small swatch of green cloth, a square about one inch in size, that is a devotional. It is also called the Scapular of the Immaculate Heart of Mary. This scapular is attributed to a private revelation by the Blessed Virgin Mary to Sister Justine Bisqueyburo in the early 1840s in Paris, France.

It was about eight months after we had done the Vancouver forest assignment that I gave it to her. I remember saying to her as I handed it over, "I know that this doesn't match all of your outfits, but please keep it with you at all times. Hopefully, the good Lord will keep you safe."

I would always see her lying on that cold slab with it nailed to her forehead. That one thing was what kept fueling my feelings of anger and hatred for Grueber. I was so totally enraged by it. His act had really managed to turn it into something that was personal to me. It felt like he was taunting and laughing at me. My anger continued to simmer for a very long time.

I hated myself for becoming like my captors. I now saw myself as one of them, a little robot that did as it was told and followed along without question. I began to talk myself back into operative mode again.

Come on, John, stop being a pussy. Are you really going to let this bunch of jerk wads get the better of you? Are you really going to let yourself be done in by these parasites? You have come this far, stop your whining for God's sake. You're whining about a few days in captivity. How in the hell do you think those guys survived being held captive in Vietnam?

They were POWs for four years while they were held at the Hanoi Hilton. They did it for four years for crying out loud, here you are whining about twelve days. Come on, get your shit together, you can do this. Don't lose your shit now, just get on with it, pull it together, man.

CHAPTER 39

Back in Prague . . .

Driesdale took me back to the hotel. I can't remember the name of it. I just know that it was a few minutes away from the Metro-Namesti Miru. Prague was made up of many small, narrow, twisty, and winding streets, some not accessible by cars. It was like a rabbit warren of little streets. The part of Prague that we were in was dark and gloomy, somewhere where tourists never ventured. In other words, a bad part of town.

The hotel had to have been a nice place as it had a canopy and *a doorman.*

We spent two to three days at the hotel while we gathered intel on where Grueber might be. Driesdale had been in the agency for a long time and was well connected worldwide. He was the one who collected the info while I collected myself together again. He allowed me that one night of self-pity, accompanied by half a bottle of whiskey, before he ordered me to get it together. He had received information from two fellow agents that had agreed to meet and speak with him at the train station. Grueber frequented this one particular pawnshop here in Prague. Driesdale also sourced out an abandoned, remote farmhouse that was for rent that was five to ten kilometers out of town. The doorman proved to be quite helpful to Driesdale, who informed him that he was originally from France, had moved away, but was looking to move back to the general area again but wanted to rent a place for a while before committing himself to purchasing a house. From the description of the house, five to ten kilometers out of town, down at the end of a dirt road, and surrounded by acres of overgrown pastureland, it appeared that it was perfect for our purposes. Driesdale spoke and met with the owner to finalize and pay for the rental.

Driesdale had such skill that he could charm anyone and fit in anywhere. It did help that he knew so many languages and could read and speak them fluently.

We found out where this particular pawnshop was and scoped out the area. Like I said, not a nice area of town, but it happened to be to our advantage.

How the streets were laid out were not straightforward. The pawnshop was located on, yet backed up against, the same street as the Metro-Namesti Miru, which happened to be a part of a huge one-way circuit or town square. This street was on the backside of the square and was shaped like an arc, with the pawnshop on the west and the road to our hotel, heading south, in the middle of the arc. At this junction, on the corner, there happened to be a bar that gave us a good view down the street of the pawnshop.

Driesdale and I decided to go into the bar one night to try to gather info on the pawnbroker. It was a small hole-in-the-wall kind of place. Dimly lit, smoke hanging heavily in the low ceiling of the room, mixing with the smell of stale beer and bodies. It was the type of place that if there were ten to fifteen people in it, it would be packed.

We casually walked up to the bar and ordered a drink. Driesdale did most of the talking as usual. He engaged the barman into a casual conversation and gradually started to ask about the pawnshop–what the hours of operation were, when it opened and closed, any little habits/routines the owner might have had, where the owner parked his car–so we'd know he was at the shop. Driesdale bought the barman a drink or two as he shot the breeze with him, inserting a subtle question here and there into the conversation. The barman was more than willing to give up what information he knew on the pawnshop. Driesdale then turned his attention to the waitress, buying her a drink, also including her in our general conversation, still peppering it with the odd question here and there. Driesdale was so smooth and subtle in the way he obtained the details from them. He had the knack of intermingling his questions into the general conversation.

We were all friends by the time that we called it a night.

CHAPTER 40

The information that we had managed to gather from the bar was complete.
We had every detail that we needed to carry out the next step in our plan.

We found out the exact hours the pawnbroker worked, that he always
left at dusk, leaving the light above the door outside on all night. He always
parked out in front of the shop so that he had less distance to walk and
was less likely to get robbed, that he lived out of town, had a wife and two
children. Not bad for a casual conversation with strangers. It's amazing just
how much information you can get out of some people.

As the word spread throughout the various agents that we were seriously
going after Grueber, it was surprising to me how many of them willingly
gave up information on him. Of course, it helped a great deal that Driesdale
knew a great number of the agents. They never gave us anything really big
or anything that would jeopardize their jobs, but what little tidbits they did
pass on to us were very helpful.

Grueber had been a person of interest to the CIA for a while. There was
a profile on all the murders and assassinations that he was believed to be
involved in. Surveillance photos had been taken of him that were about two
years old and passed along to us. It was felt that he was behind many of the
high-profile deaths, including three agents and roughly fifty people, that had
occurred over the years. At the Olympics in Munich in 1972, it was believed
that he had been gathering information for the Palestinian terrorists that
kidnapped and later killed a number of Israeli athletes. Somehow, Grueber
always managed to be somewhere in the vicinity of the murders. To me, this
was not coincidental.

We made a visit to the pawnshop. We walked in and spent a few minutes
looking around at his variety of antiques and jewelry in display cases. I
noticed that the room behind him was like a small armory. When he saw me
looking, I just shrugged and raised my eyebrows, whatever.

He was one ugly son of a bitch, let me tell you. He had nothing good going for him. I pitied his wife; either she was very shortsighted or ugly and desperate just like him. He was short, as wide as he was tall, with greasy slicked-back wisps of hair swept into a comb-over in an attempt to cover his balding head. He had more hair growing on his face than his head and gave off the odor of stale sweat mixed with cigarette smoke. What a total scuzzbag he was. He was well known for supplying weapons to anyone with the money. A real shady and unsavory character. I didn't believe that we would get much, if any, information out of him.

Driesdale showed him the photo of Grueber, telling him that he was my brother and had beaten up his wife, my sister, really bad, and we wanted to talk to him. We already knew for a fact that Grueber had been seen entering and leaving his shop on a couple of occasions recently.

As he looked at the photo, his eyes widened with fear and recognition; he was too quick in his denial of either seeing or knowing him. He flat out denied any knowledge of Grueber, backing away from us, shaking his head and hands in his vehement denial.

CHAPTER 41

Two days later, after staking out the shop from the window of the bar, we made another visit to the pawnshop. We were sitting in our compact car (what an understatement that was), waiting for the pawnbroker to leave for the day. It was approaching dusk as the pawnbroker exited the shop, locking the door, closing up for the day. We quickly drove up to the shop front and parked our car directly in front of his. Driesdale approached him with a handful of watches and pretended that he wanted to sell them as I got out of the car and opened the curbside rear door of our car. The pawnbroker tried to brush him off as he shuffled toward his own car, saying, "No, no, too late, I close for day. Come back tomorrow."

While Driesdale had him distracted with the watches, I came up to his side, pushing a gun to his ribs as I grabbed his arm, and Driesdale told him to get into the back of our car. Stealing a quick glance up and down the street, we wrestled him into the car. I shoved him on his stomach onto the backseat as Driesdale got behind the wheel. I was lying on top of him as he was struggling and trying to shout for help. I told him to be quiet, but he was not having any of that. Using my Beretta, I pistol-whipped the fat fuck on the side of his head to silence him.

Meanwhile, we'd only made it about fifty yards down the street when Driesdale stalled the car. Fuck me! I was already sweating profusely, my anxiety was off the charts, and he stalled the fucking car right in front of the bar! We really didn't need to be seen now and were doing our best to be discreet. Driesdale, remaining calm and collected, cranked the car over and over and over again. My anxiety was now rocketing toward panic mode as there were people walking in and out of the bar, walking up and down the street, and here I was lying on top of the pawnbroker on the backseat in plain view for anyone to see.

Thankfully, the little shitbox car sputtered to life, and I let out a sigh of relief as we continued down the road. I was sincerely hoping that we hadn't attracted anyone's attention because after all, if I'm not mistaken, kidnapping is illegal just about anywhere in the world.

CHAPTER 42

It didn't take long for us to cover the ten kilometers before arriving at the little farmhouse that Driesdale had already rented. It was dark now. In fact, out here where the isolated farmhouse was located, it was not just dark but pitch-black. Perfect.

The fat bastard was awake now, but more weary of us. Driesdale helped me to wrangle him out of the backseat and onto his feet. We strong-armed him into the building, sat him in an old wooden chair with arms, and tied him into place. His arms were tied to the chair arms, his legs to the chair legs. Driesdale lit two lamps to help set the mood. In actual fact, it was so that the lights would not be seen from the road. We were taking all precautions to stay unseen. The pawnbroker was quietly watchful. He knew by our demeanor that we meant business now. Little beads of sweat had broken out on his forehead; his eyes kept darting from one to the other of us as we arranged the furniture to our liking. Fear flickered in his eyes in anticipation of our next move.

The farmhouse came partially furnished with a few basic pieces of old furniture fitting for a typical farmhouse. The kitchen was clean and basic, equipped with a stove and refrigerator, wooden table, and chairs. We didn't go any farther than the kitchen as it would serve our needs.

We went about our business in silence, giving away nothing as to our intentions, adding to his already heightened level of anxiety.

Once we had everything in place, I did all the talking while Driesdale hung back in the shadows of the room. This was my show now.

I started by asking, "Where is Grueber heading to?"

He simply shook his head no.

"I know that you have some idea of where he's heading."

Again he shook his head.

"I know that he has been a regular customer of yours. So again, I ask you where he's heading." This time I pressed the Beretta to his temple.

"I don't know."

"I know that you have some idea. Now, where is he heading?"

"I don't know anything." The Beretta still pressing to his temple.

Pressing it harder, I said, "Don't lie to me again. Where is Grueber heading?"

Again he denied any knowledge.

I moved so that my eyes were level with his, holding the Beretta in his face.

"I'm going to ask one last time. If you tell us everything, we'll simply go away and just leave you here. You must be anxious to go home to your wife and two kids. now! where is grueber going?" I shouted this directly into his face.

Again he denied any knowledge.

I picked up the small can of gasoline and placed it on the table, next to the box of matches. I picked up the glass egg timer and held it up to show him.

Fear and recognition fleeted briefly across his face.

CHAPTER 43

Everything was now one big blur. Time was not important anymore. Each hour just blended in with the next. I was oblivious to the swarm of flies that now constantly hovered over my head. I was only faintly aware of Maria feeding me. I didn't bother to speak to her anymore.

I knew that I was doomed to die here sometime. I was merely just going through the motions. I had no feeling in my body. Everything had gone numb. The one fear that I did still have was not the fear of dying but the fear that I wouldn't. I tried my best to avoid thinking.

I spent less and less time in reality, preferring to stay in my memories of my life. Whether it be good memories or bad, it was still better than reality right now. I had disassociated myself from everything real.

I thought that it was maybe day 14 as we approached another little village. They all looked the same to me now. I wondered if it wasn't a movie set that we just keep circling back to. We sat and waited for dusk to arrive. Always on the outskirts of the village, hidden in the brush and undergrowth, sometimes for hours on end. I knew this routine intimately by now.

It was a recurring nightmare that kept replaying itself. As night fell, we made our way into the village and toward one of the buildings that all looked alike. I was pushed, shoved, and pulled inside, where I was taken to a room and thrown onto the floor. I knew the furniture in the main room was old and worn, that the table and chairs were battered and worn, that the illumination was poor due to either the lack of electricity or a poor supply of electricity. In these parts, it seemed that electricity was a luxury, therefore scarce commodity.

When I was thrown to the floor, I merely heard the thud my body made as it hit. I didn't feel a thing.

The chief began one of his tirades, the same questions over and over. The same accusations over and over. This continued for the majority of the night. The chief was really in a manic phase now, continuing his song and dance all night. I found myself amazed at his stamina.

In the dawn hours, through cracked, swollen, and bleeding lips, my tongue so swollen that I could barely get out my words, I said to him, "If I die, you still get nothing. Just go ahead and do what you want to do to me."

He fixed his cold, hard stare on me and said in an eerily calm, quiet, and surprisingly controlled voice, "You don't want me to do what I want to do to you."

Staring right back at him, I slurred, "I don't care anymore. But I will keep to my word, and I will get you your money because I just want to go home."

A slight grin played with the edges of his mouth.

After a few minutes go by, I was hauled to my feet and dragged into the next room.

CHAPTER 44

There sat a phone on the floor in the middle of the room. A spark of hope sprung me out of my stupor. I quickly realized that I had to gather my thoughts and wake my brain up so that I didn't fuck this up. Brutus grabbed my left hand after untying them. He placed his big rusty knife on my wrist. I was allowed to hold the phone receiver in my right. Maria came to sit at my right side. Brutus, with his mouth full of rotten teeth, was breathing right in my face, his fetid breath almost making me gag. I really struggled to stay in control, and I breathed through my mouth.

God, I hope that he doesn't bite me. What a horribly slow death that would be.

I was saying to myself, *Don't fuck this up, don't dial the wrong fucking number!*

Once again I told Maria the number as she dialed it for me. I was scrambling to get my thoughts in order. My pulse rate had gone up along with my anxiety as I was concentrating with everything I had left.

The phone rang and rang and rang. I was really anticipating receiving the wrong answer. We didn't call back when we said we would. I believed that I was shit out of luck at this point. I started to have irrational and unrealistic thoughts of how I could possibly escape.

The phone was picked up on the other end.

"Uncle John."

"Johnny, what happened? I thought you were going to call."

"Yeah, well, there was a line at the pay phone. How about the money?"

The chief was slowly working himself up by pacing to and fro in front of me. It was really distracting, and I had difficulty staying focused on the conversation.

106

"It is a lot of money that you're asking for," came his reply.

The chief was working up a good sweat now, his face beginning to turn red as his irritation was building. Maria had tears in her eyes. Thinking quickly, I changed tactics and said, "Uncle John, a friend of mine, Hans, whom I talk with often . . ."

I received a sharp slap to my face from the chief.

"Get to the fockin' munny!" he screamed. He was really wound up now; he was in my face now.

"Hans wants me to come work for him," I continued, trying to block out the chief as he continued to tell me to get to the money.

"I just might go to work for him." I really had to apply pressure now as the tension in the room was getting seriously heavy. I said, "Uncle John, does your daughter Megan still go to that nice school off of Lincoln Court?"

The chief stared at me incredulously. *What the fuck?* I held up my finger to halt his hand as he attempted to grab the receiver out of my hand. In a calm voice, I continued, "If you don't get me out of here, I'm going to talk to Hans and take a good look at Megan." Uncle John now knew that I was serious. Taking a good look at someone is code for looking through a rifle scope at someone. I continued in the same deadpan tone, "Your son Robert, does he still play soccer at that nice school? I'll take a good look at him too. I can do it, John, you know I can."

The chief's face was millimeters from my own, his breath blowing hot over my face. I looked at him and nodded my head before continuing the conversation.

"How's Sarah, that lovely wife of yours? Isn't it funny how people develop daily routines and schedules? So predictable. I like routines. I'll take a good look at her, then I'll take a good look at you." The other end of the phone remained silent as I delivered my threats. Everyone and everything became frozen in time at the anticipation of what would happen next. My heart was thumping very loud and very fast in my ears. The sweat running down my face and racing down my spine. The tension in the room was electric. I felt like I was attempting to defuse a bomb. Actually, it wasn't too far from the truth!

"What's it worth to you? Just help me out, eh?" I paused briefly before continuing. "I'll call Hans, and he won't need two to three calls to get the job done. What do you say?"

CHAPTER 45

There was a long pause, followed by a long sigh.

"We have to make arrangements for the money." The chief grabbed the phone out of my hand. Holding it away from his face, he screamed into it, "US$300,000. I call you, we set up." He threw down the receiver before stomping out of the room.

My hopes were renewed. This could just work out. Of course, Hans doesn't exist, but Uncle John doesn't know that. He doesn't know all the people that I know. I had called his bluff quite nicely.

I was rewarded by being taken back to my room, being fed and given water.

The next morning, all my hopes were dashed as I realized that we were going on the road again. I couldn't believe it.

They are going to walk me to death! I can't go any further, they will win. fuck me!

I went back to coaxing myself to continue. My body was screaming at me through its numbness. I continued to shut it out of my thoughts.

I was telling myself to take each step. I was so totally exhausted. All my concentration was on walking and breathing. I was talking myself into taking the next step and breathe, then I praised myself for accomplishing it. I had this whole conversation playing through my head.

Take one more step, go on, you can do it. What's the worst that can happen if you do? There you go, now take another step.

Take another breath. It'll hurt, yes, but take it. There, see, that wasn't that bad, you did it.

My body felt so heavy and weighed down. It was as if I was wading through a river against the current. I felt sluggish, wanting to just lie down. It would feel better then.

CHAPTER 46

Back in the farmhouse in Prague.

His constant denial was beginning to really irritate me.

I took the can of gasoline and doused his right foot with it. His eyes widened as he realized what the next step was going to be.

I told him that I would light his foot and put out the fire when the sand in the egg timer ran out. Sixty seconds. It can be a long time.

With fear clearly in his bulging eyes, he kept shaking his head back and forth, in a defiant act of denial.

"Okeydokey then," I sighed as I put the lit match to the gasoline and tipped the timer.

I stepped back as the greedy flames devoured their way through the gasoline and then started on his flesh.

The pawnbroker continued to shake his head back and forth as a high-pitched squealing sound rushed out of his gaping mouth.

The smoke at first reeked of the gasoline being vaporized by the flames then began to take on the sickening tint of seared flesh. The flames crackling and spitting, like bacon in a fry pan, as they began to taste his flesh. His squealing coming in rapid succession with each breath he took.

The sand ran out. I killed the flames. Black smoke continued to seep from his charred flesh; the skin peeled away and shriveled to a black crisp.

His breaths came rapidly now, taking on the form of sobs and gasps. His eyes were bloodshot and tear filled, his face bright red and slick with sweat. His mouth remained gaped as he greedily gulped in the air, gagging on the stench of his own seared flesh. Snot was running and mixing with his sweat and tears to drip off the end of his chin and down his shirt front. There was a dark stain at the crotch of his pants.

Breathing through my mouth, I stood directly in front of him and asked, "Where is Grueber going?"

CHAPTER 47

We came to a shallow stream. This time, Brutus dragged me into it rather than trying to stop me. He walked away, leaving me there to possibly drown for all he cared. Automatically, my mouth and throat started to work at attempting to slake my thirst. There was no quick rehydration for me now; I had gone beyond that now. My tongue had developed blisters along it. The water momentarily soothed them. The water was muddy where Brutus and gang had plodded through it, stirring up the mud to cloud it. I didn't care. I couldn't taste it anyway. I just kept sipping away, not caring what I was taking in.

When I could drink no more, I just lay there listening to the water trickle by. Half of my head remained in the water, my nose and mouth barely touching its surface, yet just enough so as I didn't drown. It felt good, and it gave the flies a new attraction to focus on.

I let myself enjoy the slight coolness of the water as it flowed over and around my body. I let thoughts, feelings, and pain flow away with it, sliding along, becoming a part of the stream. I closed my eyes and just let the sounds of the surrounding jungle to envelop me into their arms, content to listen to all the little chirps, cheeps, squeaks, pips, brrrs, and ticks going on around me.

They can leave me here. It would be okay with me if I could just die here.

CHAPTER 48

The tough old bastard lasted through three more incinerations before he finally spoke.

On the fourth attempt, I extinguished the flames that had begun to creep up his leg by now. The smoke was really thick, carrying the heavy strong odor of roasted meat. It was getting quite repulsive, even to me. Driesdale had already gone outside to throw up numerous times. He just stood in the open doorway now, turning his head to breathe in fresh air.

The pawnbroker wheezed as he whispered that Grueber was heading to France on holiday. The blackness of the night was beginning to give way to the hint of dawn as I stood in the open doorway of the farmhouse.

"Call my wife," he croaked through his sobbing.

"I will. I'll do that." I didn't.

We left the farmhouse just as the dawn light started to filter through and start a new day.

We returned to our little hotel.

CHAPTER 49

France is a big country when you are looking for someone who doesn't want to be found.

Part of the profile that had been shared with us about Grueber listed his characteristics, habits, strengths, and weaknesses.

Grueber was in his midthirties, had short blond hair and pale blue eyes. He was a West German who was handsome, with a strong body and solid build. He was well capable of taking care of himself and was known in the spy network as one of the most successful international assassins. He was feared because of how sadistic he was. He had been in the German army in the late '60s. He came from a small East German village.

His one weakness was his passion for young athletic redheaded women. Bingo! We had found the key to tracing the bastard.

Yes, France is a big country, obviously not as big as America, but still a considerable-sized haystack in which to find the proverbial needle. 'Thorn' would be a better word to use when speaking of Grueber, a thorn in my side, always there, always jabbing me as a reminder, constantly pricking at my conscious. I couldn't believe how much this one man had gotten under my skin. The emotions that he evoked in me were so raw, so fierce, and so primitive. I'd never experienced anything like it before, and it frightened me, but at the same time, I was more driven by it all. It was a dangerous state for me to be in. Emotions and murder do not mix. Mistakes could all too easily happen as my focus was not as it should be. I thanked God that my friend and colleague Driesdale had agreed to come along. I think that he could see that things might end badly for me, especially being in the frame of mind that I was currently in.

Driesdale tended to ground me. He wasn't a violent, vindictive person. He was the quiet, charming, yet unassuming kind that could talk to anyone anywhere around the world. He could extract information from anybody without them even being aware of it. He managed to appeal to both sexes:

his gentlemanly quietness to the females, his nonthreatening, intelligent manner to the males. It also helped that he was handsome, suave, and had class with a certain air of elegance about him.

As we sat enjoying a leisurely breakfast feast the morning after the farmhouse incident, we contemplated our next move. We obviously needed more details to help us to focus to where in France Grueber was heading. The wonderful food quickly disappeared. We were both ravenous. We had both skipped dinner the previous evening. The smell of charred human flesh had quelled our appetites. After downing two swift whiskeys, we had opted to go straight to bed.

In the middle of the night, I was still awake, tossing and turning. Sleep seemed to be evading me. I had had a prick of conscience and had placed a call to the pawnbroker's wife, telling her where her husband could be found. I fell asleep easily afterward.

It may seem strange that I would get a feeling of guilt. Actually, I am against unnecessary acts of violence. I don't like to kill if I don't need to. I am human after all. My conscience was eased that his family wouldn't have to be without a husband or father.

"I've been thinking, Grueber has a great passion for certain young athletic redheads, does he not?"

"That's what the intel says," I replied, wondering where he was going with this line of thought.

"It also seems to me that he is passionate to the extreme about everything that he does."

"Go on."

"I believe that our man carries out his movements with precision and a certain amount of obsession, making sure that everything goes as he would like it. He goes through great pains to make everything perfect and ruthlessly thorough. Why would he be any different when it comes to women?"

"Uh-huh."

"I believe that with his obsessive nature, he would have a strict structured routine that applies to every aspect of his life, from his grooming to his eating, to his work, and so to his women. Therefore, do you not agree that he would partake in the company of some of those such women here in Prague?"

"I believe you're right. So we look for any woman matching this description?"

"No, not any, just those who are looking for brief companionship, such as certain ladies of the night, so to speak."

CHAPTER 50

I did believe that I had lost my mind. That would explain why the world had suddenly changed. The world might be exactly as it had always been, but I saw it differently now because I had slipped over the edge of reason.

In the daylight, the walls of the green jungle were so pale they seemed to be almost white. But at night, under the light of the moon, they looked slightly greener. The foliage seemed to glow. The night was still; no breeze blew to stir the foliage, yet the green walls seemed to be swaying from side to side and back and forth.

It was disturbingly unnatural in its ceaseless motion.

In the dim light, oily shadows oozed around me. I wasn't able to shake the suspicion that I was hearing the whispers of my keepers plotting and planning my demise while they sat around the campfire. The flames distorting their faces into grotesque monsters with huge gaping mouths, laughing incessantly at me, about me, because of me.

I also knew that living among these walls of green were all sorts of creatures, always mobile, always seeking, often feeding on one another, but the jungle walls could devour them at any time it wished.

The strong act; the weak react.

Who had told me that? Someone, somewhere at some time or other. My mind was cloudy and dull. My head continued to pound away, matching the pounding of my heart.

The weak have regrets, the strong triumphs.

The weak believe in God; the strong believe in themselves.

Both the weak and the strong are a part of the food chain, and it is better to eat than be eaten.

Where had I heard that before? Maybe I'd read it somewhere.

The walls of the hungry jungle undulated rhythmically night and day. Each time one of the tree limbs or vines brushed my face, it felt like it was alive, stroking my cheek or curling a finger into my ear, tickling a nostril. I felt chilled by the contact. With each passing hour, I trembled with bewilderment, not quite able to distinguish reality from delirium.

Something was following me, stalking me. I could see its shadow still out of sight behind the thick vegetation of the jungle. The shadow brushed through the foliage that surrounded it.

The rapid beating of my heart was so loud in my ears that I barely heard Maria's gentle voice. I screamed out in alarm and sheer terror when something seized my arm. Drenched in sweat, I sat against the trunk of a tree, frantically trying to pull free from the creature that had finally attacked.

Maria's face and voice soothed me back to a semblance of reality. I recognized a friendly face. She gave me water, much-needed water. I couldn't remember the last time that I had peed. She poured some water over my head. I was suddenly aware of how hot I felt. My eyes burned and felt dry in their sockets. The water cooled me a little. Too little, too late.

Maria tried her best to keep me with her, comforting me, telling me that I was seeing things that were not there. I half believed her; it took so much energy.

But I knew the thing had retreated farther into the green maze.

These walls of vegetation felt like the walls of a trap, and I was caught in the middle.

CHAPTER 51

I'd lost all concept of time, so I didn't know for certain how long I had been trapped in the nightmare that my state of delirium had created. I just knew that all of a sudden, they seemed to be a little concerned about me. They gave Maria permission to feed me a little more, to keep me better hydrated. They really had begun to whisper and look at me while they sat around the fire at night. I think that my crazy behavior had actually scared them. Some of them would cross themselves and offer a few words up to the sky after they had looked at me. The chief kept getting into huddles of whispered conversation with Maria. I suspected that he was scared that I would die before he got his money. He only needed me to survive until the money was in his hands. He didn't care about me. I knew this and didn't really give a shit. I watched as the vultures circled in the sky above me daily. Not long now. I was hanging on the very brink of death. I wished that I could get it over with. The game had grown old a long time ago many miles back in the jungle.

I sat there tied to a tree, just laughing to myself as I thought and rambled out loud what I was going to do to all of them before I died.

I was going to go out in a blaze of glory. I was going to poke their eyes out with a stick, making them blind before I hacked them up with one of the machetes. I was going to jump one of them and grab his gun and shoot until I ran out of bullets. I was going to tie them all up and slowly torture them with a thousand cuts. When we came across the next stream, I would drown them and leave them there floating like the scum they were. Of course, this was all talk and fantasy on my part. My body was barely functioning, although I did feel more lucid since the increase in my water rations. I don't know if I was grateful or resentful. I just didn't know anymore.

116

I was unable to walk by myself, so now when we were trekking through the jungle, I had a sapling run through behind my back. They retied my hands behind me. This way, they could carry and drag me along more easily. I no longer slowed them down. I had ceased to feel by now. When they hit me or burned me, I no longer felt it or even bothered to flinch anymore. I was already dead. For most of the time now, I lived in my memories, where it was safe and secure and untouched deep within my mind.

CHAPTER 52

Back in Prague . . .

The barman in our hotel proved to be a mine of information. He told Driesdale where the majority of the hookers strutted their stuff and the name of a couple of high-end hotels where the high-end girls frequented. The barman was very sympathetic toward our plight; his sister had experienced something similar to my fictional wife. His sister had blond hair and blue eyes so wouldn't be of any help to us.

So we hit the maze of narrow, twisting, gloomy streets of Prague's sleazy side.

The barman had warned us to watch ourselves as this was not a desirable part of the city. He even asked us if we had protection; he didn't mean condoms either.

There were about thirty places in all that we could visit and probably come across what we were looking for. The places were a mixture of clubs, bars, low-end motels, and a couple of actual strip clubs. All of them were seedy, rundown establishments that you felt like you needed to wipe your feet on the way out. This was the true heart of all crimes and drugs, both for trafficking, sales, and use. Money could buy you anything in this armpit of a city. Why was it that such places existed in every city around the world? It was truly disturbing to me. Absolutely anything could be had for a price; life was cheap.

We had to be cautious as we didn't want to attract any attention to ourselves. These people had their own grapevine, and word would travel fast that two American guys were seeking redheads and asking questions. We thought it best if we didn't always do the approaching. We would pay someone twenty dollars to go and show the redhead in question the photo of Grueber and see if she knew him or had seen him. You could usually tell by the facial expressions and body language of the woman whether she had seen him or not.

In one particular grungy club, we had learned that they had a dancer who fit the description of the type of female we were seeking.

The front door opened into a shabby hallway, dimly lit, with yellowed wallpaper peeling back at its edges. The ever-present odor–a mix of sweat, vomit, and pee–assaulting your nostrils the minute you opened the door. At the end of the hallway was a counter, behind which sat a bored bouncer. He was a big boy, even under the hundred fifty extra pounds that he carried, his shoulders seeming to fill the width of the hallway. He sat on a stool with arms folded across his ample chest, a black T-shirt stretched over his bulk. His head was bald, and his facial expression was a poor attempt at intimidation that ended up looking like simple boredom. The lit cigarette dangling from his lips dropped a dusting of ash onto his T-shirt. Driesdale handed him a wad of cash. Happy with that, he opened the door to his right and allowed us to enter the inner sanctum of the strip club.

Like every other strip club that we had previously visited, the room was loud, dark, and smoky. The layout, identical to the others, gave a sense of déjà vu. A lighted stage was the centerpiece of the room. There were tables scattered around the stage and around the rest of the room. The tiny bar, with its watered-down but high-priced drinks, gave the impression that it had been shoved into a corner out of the way so as not to distract the attention away from the stage.

A handful of tired-looking men occupied seats around the stage. They held drinks in their hands, their faces directed toward the dancer on the stage. They looked without seeing as the dancer performed her pitiful routine out of time with the loud thumping music.

The "dancer" was a tall, skinny, almost emaciated slip of a thing. She had no noticeable curves that I could see. She had bleached-blond hair that hung in greasy threads around her head and three inches of dark roots showing at her scalp. Her face wore the deadpan expression of somebody high on drugs, oblivious to her surroundings. She couldn't have been but eighteen yet looked twice the age. She looked well worn and tired out.

CHAPTER 53

The petite waitress, wearing an obvious false smile affixed to her lips, brought us our watery drinks and asked if we needed anything else. Driesdale engaged in conversation with her while I glanced back to the stage.

The new dancer with raven hair reminded me of a naughty librarian by the way she was dressed. Her hair was pinned up. She wore black-rimmed glasses, a dingy white shirt, black skirt, and stilettos. The tempo of the thumping music started off slow and quickly increased. After unpinning her hair, she tossed her head to allow her raven tresses to fling out before settling down her back. Pursing her red glossy lips into an exaggerated pout, she yanked the white blouse open to reveal a lacy low-cut bra. Just as I was beginning to think that she had what it took, she ruined the image by yanking off her shirt, followed by her skirt. You could hear the ripping of Velcro letting go, totally spoiling the moment. A matching lacy G-string accompanied the lacy bra. What had happened to the slow, tantalizing striptease of old? It was as if these girls had to get down to business as quick as possible. Very off-putting for me.

Turning her back to the room, she bent her knees, and as she thrust her ass in the air, she ripped away the G-string to reveal everything that the good Lord had given her. Believe me, she hadn't been at the front of the line when God was giving those out! She continued to swirl and sway in an attempt at a sensual and primal rhythm. It failed to work for me.

I turned my attention back to our table, pretending to take a sip of my watery whiskey, when the petite waitress returned with a redheaded girl in tow. She was obviously a young teenager as her figure had yet to fill out from its boyish build. Her skin was milky pale, dotted with an odd tattoo. She went by the name of Domino, hence the tattoo of a double-six domino tile on her shoulder. Her face was heart shaped and quite pretty. She looked like a little elf. A black eye stood out from her pale complexion despite the attempt to cover it with makeup. She was jittery and uneasy. I wasn't sure if she was nervous or strung out on some drug or other. Maybe it was both. She avoided eye contact as Driesdale spoke to her. The sheer look of terror that washed over her face when Driesdale showed her the photo told me that she knew Grueber. She confirmed that she had been with him about a week ago and that he had roughed her up some. She was a streetwalker and thought that Grueber to be the devil himself and hoped that she would never encounter him again. Driesdale handed her a wad of cash as he thanked her for her time.

At least we now had confirmation that Grueber had visited the area. Our thoughts had proved to be correct. But we were still no closer to his intended destination in France.

The next few days proved futile in our hunt for information of Grueber. Finding ourselves totally repulsed at the thought of having to visit yet another den of iniquity, we decided to check out the high-class hotels in the area as suggested by the barman. It was a treat to visit such an establishment. We settled ourselves in at the lounge of one such hotel, enjoying the total change of atmosphere. I was sick of feeling filthy at the end of each night that we had visited the sleazy part of town. I had not derived one iota of pleasure during our numerous visits to sleaze town. I, like the next man, enjoyed viewing tits and ass, but not when those tits and asses were so pathetically tired and worn out. The bodies were empty shells like zombies, just aimlessly gyrating to some beat or other.

CHAPTER 54

On the second night of our hotel bar vigil, at the end of nearly two weeks in Prague, our patience finally paid off.

We'd been in the lounge of this one hotel (I forget the name probably because I couldn't pronounce it) when a man and woman walked in from the direction of the elevators. The man looked to be in his midfifties, well dressed, with impeccable grooming, and had the look of some kind of businessman. The woman draped on his arm was stunning. Equally as well dressed, impeccable grooming, a certain elegance about her. She had long, curly red hair and ruby-red lips. I had to pick my tongue up off the floor so as not to attract attention to us. She managed to capture the attention of everyone else in the room.

The man bought her a glass of champagne before kissing her hand, bidding her a good night, and left her sitting alone at the bar.

Watching her sitting there conversing with the barman, I couldn't help but think that if she had crossed Grueber's path, despite being a little older than his usual preference of teenagers, she would have surely captured his attention. When she slowly swiveled around on her chair, she slowly perused the room over the rim of her champagne glass.

Her eyes fell on Driesdale. He held up his drink in a salute to her before turning on his charming smile. She returned the salute and smile. The maestro was at work!

After refilling her glass, she glided over to where we sat, waited to be invited to sit and join us, then folded herself into one of the plush leather armchairs at our table. I was entranced by her enchanting smile and must have looked like a right idiot to her as I continued to stare. Obviously used to being looked at, she started talking to Driesdale. After a few words were exchanged, she began to speak in English. Finding my manners, I apologized to her, saying that her beauty captivated me. She smiled and thanked me.

"We will pay you for your time," I said.

"What? Pay me for my time, I don't understand." It wasn't that she was offended by our implication; she was taken by surprise.

"I have a couple of important questions that I need to ask you."

"I still don't . . ." Before she could finish, I placed the photo of Grueber on the table between us. She flinched away from it and started to stand while shaking her head.

"no, no, I cannot . . ." Panic and terror were evident both on her face and in her voice. Driesdale steadied her by placing his hand gently on her forearm, urging her to sit back down. She was visibly uncomfortable. I leaned toward her, and in a quiet voice, I said, "Ma'am, I give you my personal guarantee that you will never again encounter this evil man."

She relaxed a little yet still had that questioning look in her eyes. Driesdale related the story about him being my brother-in-law who had beaten his wife, my beloved sister, within inches of death and that we wanted to find him and take care of him.

"By take care of . . . ?" she asked.

"Eliminate," I replied.

Letting out a big sigh, she told us that, yes, she had had the misfortune to be with Grueber, that he had choked her and beaten her. She then revealed the bruises on her neck. They looked to me to be fresher than a week old as she claimed. Neither Driesdale nor I pointed that out to her. She told us that she had threatened him with a visit from her three brothers. He had merely laughed at her, saying that they would have to travel a long way to find him as he was going to Marseille for a vacation. Jackpot! The tidbit of information that we needed.

CHAPTER 55

The world continued to be off-kilter. Everything remained distorted, making it difficult to know what was real and what was the feverish insanity-talking.

The walls of the jungle continued to undulate rhythmically although the night was windless.

A moon sailed the heavens, slowly navigating across the sea of stars.

Each tree rose high, spreading its crooked fingerlike branches, seeming to claw at the moon as if reaching out to try to capture it and drag it down into the endless mass of the vast green canopy. As I lay slumped against a tree trunk, gazing up at the night sky, I realized that my thinking was really fucked up. Bizarre ran wildly through my head. My eyes and brain were playing tricks on me by making things out of ordinary shadows, my brain matrixing all these nonexistent creatures that were looming in the darkness of the foliage. I held whole conversations with myself, asking if what I was seeing was real or imagined. The only thing that I can honestly remember being lucid about is Maria. Her concern for me grew by the hour, but nothing could be done as her actions were closely monitored by the chief. I kept reassuring her that I was okay, that I hadn't completely lost it. To be honest, it was far easier to give in to the insane thoughts and conversations as I didn't exert half the energy as I did to stay lucid and coherent. I was actually pretty amused at most of the crap that was running through my head. Where does this stuff come from? Deep inside, I was still in control. I was just playing along, very happy to let them think that I was loco.

One particular night, though, really stood out for me. There was a thunderstorm, one of those storms that had the "fill the entire sky" lightning and deafening "right above you" thunder that you could feel reverberate through your entire body. Normally, I don't like these kinds of storms, but I found the storm to be highly amusing. I was singing along to the storm with Tchaikovsky's *1812 Overture*, the thunder being the cannons, the rain the musical notes, me waving my arms around being the conductor of the entire show. During that time, I felt empowered, alive, unafraid of anything out there, enjoying the rain thrash against my body. It felt good to let it all go. By the end of the storm, I was totally spent. I sat there breathing heavily yet was left feeling invigorated. I had just been scrubbed clean both internally as well as externally by the thrashing rain and felt revitalized, calmer, and peaceful. They left me alone that night, and I slept.

They didn't bother to keep my hands tied during the nights now as they believed that I was totally insane and no threat to them. They knew that I couldn't run off as I couldn't walk. I was happy to let them keep thinking that.

CHAPTER 56

Weaving awkwardly, I hobbled along. Jolts of pain shooting up and down my legs, my shoulders and arms were on fire, along with any and all many other injuries joining in with their protests at being asked to move. I tangled with a wall of saplings and thick brush and lost my balance, falling face-first onto the rain-soaked earth. My face was not only bruised but now muddied.

Keeping close to the jungle floor, stumbling clumsily along branches and vines grabbing and slapping my face, I risked a glance over my shoulder. I could see no sign of the faceless man who pursued me. The torrential rain and mounting gloom making visibility near impossible.

I had absolutely no idea where I was going or from where I had come. I just knew that I had to keep moving. After another few minutes, I stopped and listened for any sign of the man. The sound of the rain and my heavy, labored breathing made it difficult to hear anything. It took several seconds before I made out the soft crunching of brush. He was moving stealthily but steadily toward me.

Do I hide, or do I run?

Through the gloom and rain, I made out the shadow of the man. I quickly realized that there was nowhere to hide. The darkness was at the moment my friend, but my injuries were also my enemy. Crawling forward on hands and knees, I waited until I reached thicker undergrowth before I dared to stand upright again.

Ignoring the searing burn from the gunshot wound, I barreled ahead through the trees and vines, using my forearms to protect my face from the whipping branches.

The ground was uneven but became increasingly so with rotting vegetation covering various holes and roots. The ground dipped unexpectedly, and I failed to see the exposed rock. My foot caught the solid rock, and I found myself tumbling down a steep embankment, landing heavily on my back in the middle of a slow-running stream. My head snapped against a rock with dizzying force, the wind thrust out of my lungs on impact.

Trying desperately to suck air back into my lungs and fighting off unconsciousness, I got my arms and legs all going in the same direction. Somewhere above me, I heard the crunch and cracking of branches as something moved among them. Oblivious to all the pain, I drove myself forward along the banks of the stream.

Suddenly, from behind me and to my right, I heard the crack of gunfire, followed by the buzz of a bullet cutting through the air. Immediately to my right, the bark of a tree splintered. Whirling my head around, I made out the silhouette of the man now only about a hundred yards away. Driven by a new intense urgency, I pushed forward.

Another bullet zipped past my right ear, slicing into a tree only inches from my head.

It was probably a totally irrational thought, but I could see no alternative so kept following alongside the stream. Keeping my vision focused forward as I stumble on.

My eyes remained fixed on the ground in front of me as I tried to dodge the holes and roots and rocks. I realized that the ground was changing and lifted my head just in time to see the stream disappear.

CHAPTER 57

It fell away. I dropped to my knees, inching forward until I found myself peering down into darkness. I could hear water falling away and beneath me. It was impossible to tell how far down it went. From behind I heard the telltale cracking of branches again. I lay there trying to weigh my options but quickly realized that there were none. More rustling at my back.

Turning my body so that I would face the rock, I eased my body over the ledge. Moss and moisture turned every rock and crevice slick and treacherous. There was no sure footing, no dependable handholds. I grappled around blindly among the loose stones until I found what I hoped to be a reasonable grip. My legs barely able to support me as they trembled with pain and exhaustion. I moved painstakingly slow, working my way down inch by inch.

A small rock clattered past just a few feet from my face. Looking up, I could make out the silhouette again of the man. The next rock smashed just above my head, showering me with dust and stones. It took all my concentration to keep my grip. Another rock clattered down, followed by another one. This one hit me squarely on my left shoulder, causing me to lose my grip on the rock face, and I found myself falling, arms and legs flailing as the air rushed by.

I hit the water hard, air exploding from my lungs. Everything went black.

I didn't know that I was dreaming, let alone that I had fallen asleep. I woke as I screamed out in the dream. Still feverish, hallucinatory, the borders between reality and dream were still very blurry and confusing. My heart thundered in my ears. My breath came short and rapid. The longer the memory of the dream lingered, the more it disturbed me. I quickly ran my hands over my body, checking for gunshot wounds and other new injuries.

I was relieved when I found none.

Scrubbing my hands across my face, I realize that it was dawn. Again I experienced that very briefest of moments of elation followed quickly by the feeling of dread. I'd made it through another night, but could I survive another day?

CHAPTER 58

Agents like Grueber were known as ghosts. You could always sense him but never see him. Then something would happen, and he was gone, unseen and silent, like ghosts. This man was at the very top of the international assassin food chain. He was the best there was. He had made a career and living out of what he did. He was damn good. If I didn't despise him so much, I would admire him. He had made an art out of being a ghost. His superior intelligence enabled him to plan and prepare and execute meticulously without problems. He always worked alone, never letting anyone get close to him. He was like a robot, no emotions, rigid self-control, impeccable attention to detail, precise execution of tasks. He was the great white who survived in the worst cesspool of the underworld; he was the big fish. His network of contacts was immense, reaching to every corner of the world. Once he was on to someone, he was both ruthless and relentless. His success rate was 100 percent. Nobody ever escaped him.

We were playing a high-stakes game, knowing full well that we were hunting someone who was far superior to us. There was no room for mistakes. Word would definitely get back to Grueber that we were looking for him, and he would, in turn, be looking for us. We really had to step up our game in order to be successful. Not only were we the hunter, we were also the hunted. That's quite an intimidating position to be in and could easily be a distraction and ultimately our downfall. We felt that our only chance of being successful would be the element of surprise. That was going to prove to be extremely difficult. 'Hypervigilance' was an understatement. To stay ahead, we had to take things slowly, cautiously, be meticulous in our planning and preparations.

CHAPTER 59

We took the next available flight to Paris. From Charles de Gaulle Airport, we boarded a train headed for Marseille.

Train travel was easier for the likes of us as you could easily carry a concealed weapon, having no security checks like they had at airports. There was also no paper trail as you could buy a ticket with cash and not have to supply any means of identification. It took us longer to make the journey than if we had flown, but we felt that this way made more sense. Airports were generally watched more than the train stations. Hopefully, this would be to our advantage.

Conversation was kept to a minimum as we traveled across France. I spent a great deal of time looking out of the window as the scenery went by, but I didn't really see it as I was too engrossed in my thoughts. I was planning and making preparations in my head. One thing was for certain: our handguns were now very inadequate, and I desperately wanted to get better armed. Driesdale came up with the ruse that we were on vacation and wanted to do a little grouse hunting, hence the need for bigger guns.

The journey took about four hours. Exiting the train in Marseille station, our instincts took over as we automatically started to scan the crowds for familiar faces and any dubious-looking individuals. Remember, we were now the hunted. We tried to appear casual as we scanned our surroundings, taking in as much detail as we could. Our training at the farm makes it second nature to be fully aware of your surroundings.

Marseille Train Station is a fantastic feat of architecture and stonework, with its high glass-domed ceilings. The exterior is more impressive than its interior, with white stone walls complete with intricate carvings, cornices, and moldings. It gives the feel of a grand palace as a broad stone stairway sweeps you up to the grand entrance.

I didn't have the time to appreciate it. We carried our own luggage rather than allow one of the many porters to handle it for us.

We had been extremely vigilant on the train, not leaving each other alone for any length of time, restricting our movements, not wanting to make targets out of ourselves or put ourselves in any vulnerable positions. So I really had to pee. Locating the bathroom was easy throughout Europe as they always had the distinguishing signs posted along with the WC signs.

Driesdale was uneasy at having to spend any more time than was necessary in the building. But nature calls. As we nonchalantly moved among the crowd, Driesdale noticed a man in a herringbone coat who seemed to be taking an interest in us. About fifty feet from the bathroom entrance were some newer-looking plastic seats that really didn't fit with the rest of the decor but were an attempt at modernization. Picking up a newspaper, Driesdale occupied a plastic seat, giving him a direct view to the men's room entrance.

After entering one of the stalls, I closed but didn't lock the door. I sat on the toilet and pulled my feet off the floor. Men, unlike women, go into a bathroom to take care of business and come immediately out. We don't tend to hang around to chat. I sat, waiting and listening for a couple of minutes before it emptied out, leaving only me in the stall. It had gone pretty quiet, so it was easy for me to hear the door opening slowly. I then heard the sound of expensive leather shoes pacing back and forth across the tiled floor. I was alert and ready, my senses alerting me. When the door to my stall was pushed open, I immediately kicked it hard, so it closed bouncing back, banging into the man. The force of the door caused the man to drop the gun in his hand the same time that Driesdale appeared from behind him, forcing him into the stall. It was a little cramped with three of us in the stall.

In French, Driesdale says, "Give me one good reason why I shouldn't kill you now."

I picked up the fallen gun and pocketed it. I was in no mood for a shoot-out in the men's bathroom in the middle of a Marseilles station that was crawling with both metropolitan police and gendarmes. Not a wise move. The man answered Driesdale, who looked over to me and shook his head. He had the man pinned up against the wall. I asked in my best French accent, "Parlez-vous Anglais?" He just stared at me with cold eyes and an expressionless face.

I took out my pocket knife and rammed it into his arm, just up past the bicep. "Do you understand this?" I asked in English.

Driesdale again gave him fifteen seconds to tell us whom he was working for.

"*I work for the same people that you do. I can help you find what you're looking for.*"

"*Bullshit. You're a fucking liar,*" *I said as I twisted the knife in his arm before pulling it out and wiping it on his coat. I frisked him before I exited the stall. I heard Driesdale tell him that he was to wait, count to two hundred, and then meet us later at a certain café. As I was washing my hands in one of the sinks, Driesdale started to primp and preen in the mirror, not taking his eyes off the man now slumped in the stall. He told him that if he should show himself again unexpectedly, then he would die. He painstakingly took his time to vainly preen his mustache as he spoke to the man. He continued to tell him that he needed to stop squirming as it was making his friend here nervous.*

I told him that we needed to get going, and in his cool, unshakable manner, he said, "I am not leaving here looking like I've been in a fight."

Before exiting the bathroom, I advised the man to get his arm seen to as I couldn't remember the last time that I had cleaned my knife. We composed ourselves before we exited the bathroom, picked up our cases from where we'd left them. The gendarmes were swarming all over the station. You can spot them a mile away with their silly white pillbox-type hats. We hastily hailed a cab. Driesdale told the driver to go to the Hotel Des Etats-Unis (Hotel United States). Driesdale was a much-traveled man and knew an impressive number of places and people. His immense knowledge of people, places, and languages never failed to astound me. He even knew all the different dialects that belonged to each region in each country and was fluent in them all.

CHAPTER 60

The hotel was impressive in its age and elegance. Having a huge lobby area and reception desk, concierge service, with beautiful soft plush leather couches sitting on luxuriously thick carpets. It was classic, stylish, and smelled of old money and history. After we had checked in, it was midafternoon. We hadn't eaten in a while, so we decided to go out to one of the many bistros just down the street. After eating, we went back to the hotel, where Driesdale asked the concierge where we would be able to buy some hunting equipment. He gave him our cover story about going grouse hunting. Armed with a street map, we set off in search of this exclusive gentlemen's outdoor outfitter.

Riding through the maze of narrow streets with their small square stone houses, we went around the old harbor, only able to catch glimpses of scenery when breaks in the tall walls allowed. A cathedral stood proudly on surrounding hills, with a huge steeple and statue of the Virgin Mary. The main street that circled the marina was full of enormous outside cafés and exclusive and expensive shops. It seemed that the ancient could live side by side with the old, yet neither was too happy about all the new.

Once inside the shop, the owner showed us a number of shotguns. I was immediately drawn to the select few rifles that he carried. Driesdale went through the story about grouse hunting. The shop owner looked over to me and said, "You don't hunt grouse with a rifle, sir." Smart guy, obviously knows his guns.

"Oh, I do all different kinds of hunting. I'm somewhat of a collector of fine guns, and these fine pieces caught my eye."

Driesdale purchased a Beretta shotgun that came in a beautiful satin-lined case, along with ammunition in keeping with our story. I couldn't resist buying a 7 mm Belgian bolt-action rifle with scope and wooden stock. A truly exceptional piece.

I felt more at ease now that we were better equipped.

I sighted in the rifle in our room. I placed it across two chairs, picked a target about fifty to sixty feet away through the window, and kept adjusting the scope until I could see the same thing out of both the barrel and scope. It takes time but is relatively easy if you know how. We were ready for our prearranged meeting with our friend from the bathroom the next day at a bistro.

I wanted to see this bistro and get a general feeling of its layout. I really wanted to find a rooftop vantage point. We acted like tourists on vacation. I carried a cheap camera with no film in it. Looking around outside of the bistro, I noticed a For Rent sign in a fourth-floor window. Telling Driesdale to take a seat inside the window, I crossed the street and entered the building with the sign. I found the landlord, who happened to speak English, thank God, and asked him about the room. He showed me to a vacant apartment on the fourth floor. I took a look around and then asked if I could come back the next day to show it to my girlfriend, who was really picky and hard to please. Understanding completely, he smiled and agreed.

I met Driesdale in the bistro, and we ate while we discussed our plan of action. I told Driesdale that I wouldn't be with him at the meeting but that I'd be close by, watching. I told him that if things didn't feel right, he should signal to me by slowly leaning back in his chair, stretching his arms above his head, and then clasping his hands behind his head.

"Why would I go through all that?"

"To avoid flying broken glass."

"Oh . . . so you intend to kill him then?"

"Maybe, maybe not. We'll see tomorrow."

CHAPTER 61

We were to meet the man for brunch, so we got there ahead of time, scouting out the area first to see if anything or anyone looked suspicious. I was carrying my rifle in its case and was wondering how I was going to explain it to the landlord. Also, how was I to explain the absence of my girlfriend?

I needn't have worried. When I got to the apartment, there was no sign of the landlord, but the door was unlocked. I immediately became suspicious and on full alert. We had arranged the time after all. I cautiously opened the door of the apartment; my heart was hammering loudly in my chest, my palms sweaty with anxiety. To my relief, there was a note on the table. It said to help ourselves and to take as long as we needed. Perfect!

Driesdale had already taken position in his window seat across the street. I arranged the furniture and myself just inside the window of the apartment. You always want to stay back from the window, not showing the gun in any way so as not to be seen, not like they do in the movies.

The man finally showed up twenty minutes late. He was obviously nervous and very uncomfortable, fidgeting on the spot as he remained standing, avoiding the other window seat. I could see them talking back and forth, then Driesdale slid an envelope across the table. The contents seemed to surprise the man. I was watching the interaction all the time through my scope. It lasted about four minutes, and then the man abruptly left.

Driesdale signaled to me that it was good. We hailed a cab and went to a nearby park to discuss the meeting.

Apparently, the man got agitated as Driesdale pointed out to him that he was there to answer our questions, not to ask them. When he asked Driesdale why he should answer any of our questions, he told him that it was better than dying, at which point the man became squirrelly. Driesdale said that he was obviously a rookie in the field as he was way too nervous to be an experienced agent.

The man told Driesdale that he had been hired to follow us and find out what we were up to. He also said that we were very vulnerable in this particular situation. Driesdale then told him that no, he was the vulnerable one as I was on the rooftop watching through a rifle scope and not to make any wrong moves. This was what the man reacted to, not what was in the envelope as I had thought. He derived no information from the brief meeting, but Driesdale, being Driesdale, couldn't help but taunt the man before his departure. He told him that he was easy to find and that if we ever saw him again, his family would receive a very distressing letter describing his death. To further tease him, he said that I wanted to know if he had gotten his arm seen to like I had suggested. It was at this point that the man had abruptly left.

The only news that we had attained was that the CIA was hiring outside sources to track us, obviously as it was cheaper than using our own agents. This was a little unsettling to us but just served to remind us what type of game we were involved in.

Basically, we had wasted an entire day on this jackass.

So this meant that we were back to hitting the clubs again. Only this time, the odds had changed from one hundred skanks and one beautiful woman in Prague to one hundred beautiful women and just a handful of skanks here in France. The odds were definitely in our favor.

That night, we hit five high-end gentlemen's clubs. Not a redhead was to be found.

CHAPTER 62

The next day, as we hung around in the vast lobby, sipping cappuccinos, relaxing, and reading the tabloids, Driesdale, in his debonair manner, struck up various conversations with different guests. His talent for schmoozing among a crowd was amazing. I don't know how he does it. Most of the time, people are unaware of just how much personal information they give away in the course of a casual conversation with strangers. That's how Driesdale worked the crowd. They were totally unaware that they were being manipulated into divulging information that he was seeking. They were too busy being dazzled by his enigma and charm.

At some point during the day, he slipped the concierge a generous wad of money, asking him to seek out the most exclusive dating agencies. He told the concierge that the women had to be so beautiful that they would impress his mother. He also asked that they be redheaded, that we would wine and dine them, but not here at the hotel. He asked that he make a reservation for the following night at an expensive restaurant.

"We are on vacation, time is no problem. I have complete faith in you, my man."

I didn't like all this waiting around. I was impatient and anxious to be on the move, doing something instead of just sitting and chatting. I wanted information like the previous day. I wanted answers to questions I didn't even know. I was really antsy.

My grief was smothering my common sense, causing me not to think clearly. I was totally irrational in my thinking and in the things that I wanted to do.

Driesdale sat me down later that evening and bluntly confronted me with my behavior. Because it was Driesdale, I took it well. He helped me to refocus and to get me back on track.

The following afternoon, we were once again sitting in the lounge area doing the same thing. Driesdale called the concierge over and asked if he had been successful in acquiring the information that he had requested.

We learned that we had reservations for dinner at 8:00 p.m. at this five-star restaurant in the marina. This marina was large and impressive with its huge selection of big expensive boats. It was known to be frequented often by Aristotle Onassis and his yacht. I'm impressed. I wondered to myself if he was in town and if he knew Grueber. I wouldn't be at all surprised, but it was highly unlikely.

Later on in the early evening, as we were sitting in the lounge at our hotel, there were two gorgeous women sitting at the bar, sipping martinis. One of them was a redheaded beauty with sorrel-colored hair, perfect creamy skin, and curves in all the right places. Their clothes, hair, makeup, and shoes all screamed of big money and class. The concierge signaled that these were our dates. Wow, surely these beauties didn't need to be hookers. They looked like they came from aristocratic families. It was pretty hard for me to believe.

We looked over, caught their eye, and smiled. They returned our smile.

And . . . action. We were on.

Casually we got up and walked over to them and asked if we might join them in a drink.

After asking if they spoke English, we introduced ourselves. The redhead was Anastasia; her equally gorgeous friend, Yvette. We fell easily into idle chitchat. Actually, Driesdale did most of the talking. The rest of us mostly listened. Driesdale was a true master in the art of meaningless and idle conversation.

We went to dinner at the restaurant, which was grand and luxurious. I felt out of place and didn't really enjoy the food as I couldn't identify half of what I was eating. In my opinion, most French food tends to be slimy, and I definitely don't do slimy!

I turned to Anastasia next to me and asked if there was anywhere that we could get a hamburger. It took her a couple of seconds and hand signals to comprehend before she collapsed into a fit of giggles. God, she was gorgeous, like a goddess. I found myself mesmerized by her sheer beauty and had to keep kicking myself to stay focused.

When we had done eating, Driesdale suggested that we all go for a walk. The three of us looked at him as if he was crazy. It was a cool and windy evening, requiring coats to be worn. Yvette suggested that we instead go some place where it was warm. We were all in agreement with this. They took us to their apartment.

CHAPTER 63

Their apartment was in a beautiful building overlooking the marina. By French standards for apartments, this one was like a hotel penthouse suite. The decor matched their appearances. A great deal of money had gone into furnishing this large space. It was very opulent in all white and gold and crystal.

Yvette led Driesdale to one of the three couches that sat in front of a huge fireplace. Anastasia led me into her bedroom.

She leaned her body in close to mine and reached for my tie. I gently grasped her hand to stop her. She had a puzzled look on her face.

"I need your help. I will financially reimburse you for your time."

"But I thought that you wanted . . ."

I cut her off by placing my finger on her lips to hush her before I led her to a small sitting area by a window.

I then went on to explain the story of my sister who had married this man who was very cruel and brutal toward her. The last time that he had beaten her, she had died. I needed to find this man. We talked for a while about people and their relationships and behaviors and what drives people to act the way they do. She was very sincere and open with me. She had a soft, gentle way about her.

"I need your help. I need to know if you've seen this man." I pulled out the envelope that contained the photo of Grueber. This time she was the one who grabbed my wrist to stop it.

"I don't need to see a picture. I know the man whom you seek. He is German, blond hair, blue eyes. Handsome. Very strong. An evil man." She then opened her silk blouse to show me the marks that Grueber had left on her. My stomach roiled with nausea as I looked at the burn marks on her breasts. Silently I closed her blouse again.

140

Anastasia was trembling with the memories; tears welled in her eyes. I gently placed my arms around her and held her to me. We stayed that way, unspeaking, for a few minutes. Silent tears were now running down her face. Looking into her eyes, I said, "I can't undo what he has already done to you, but I promise you that I will do everything in my power to make sure that he will never come back to hurt you again."

Silently she nodded her head as she began to regain her composure. I started to take money from my wallet.

"No, I don't want payment from you, just the promise of my safety." We looked into each other's eyes for a minute or two before I kissed her on her forehead and stood up.

I heard raised voices from the next room and realized that Yvette was screeching at Driesdale.

"You pig, you don't want sex with me. You don't find me attractive?"

"Actually, no. You are actually beginning to bore me."

Anastasia stepped in to stop Yvette from physically attacking Driesdale. He was his usual unruffled self.

"You leave now," said Anastasia as she continued to hold back the wildcat that Yvette had turned into.

"Ladies . . . ," Driesdale's parting comment, ever the gentleman.

I relayed what Anastasia had told me about Grueber. She was with him four days prior to our meeting. She also recalled that he had mentioned something about a fiesta in Spain. She thought it was the Festival San Lorenzo.

Of course, Driesdale knew of it. It is held annually in early July, in Madrid, Spain.

CHAPTER 64

We flew from Marseille to Madrid. We knew that we had only missed him by four days. We were definitely on the right track.

After checking into three hotels, we settled into one of them. We then again went about making our inquiries and contacts. Again Driesdale handed over a big wad of money to the concierge of the hotel, asking about high-class dating services. Once again we were surrounded by many beautiful women, only they were nearly all raven haired with olive skin.

We had a number of "dates" with some truly magnificent-looking women, but we had yet to obtain any clues. No one had even seen or recognized Grueber.

Just as we were beginning to doubt our decision in coming here, the concierge attracted our attention to two women at the lounge bar.

One woman looked to be in her midforties but was immaculately and stylishly dressed. The other woman was younger, probably half her age, equally as immaculate as her friend.

We asked the waiter to invite the two beauties over to us so that we might buy them a drink.

Neither Driesdale nor I were feeling particularly optimistic about this encounter. But I'd much rather spend time with two beautiful women than alone with just Driesdale.

True to form, Driesdale turned on the charm, and we acted out our little charade for what felt like the umpteenth time. It was getting a little old.

One thing that they teach you at the farm is patience. Patience pays off in the end. I had my own set of rules that I lived by. It was the four Ps: planning, preparation, patience, and perseverance. These four principles had served me well and sometimes saved my ass through my time with the agency.

We decided to remain where we were in the lounge as we were somewhat tucked away in a corner with not much traffic passing by. Plus, the big armchairs were so comfortable, and their high backs afforded us some modicum of privacy.

Nonchalantly, Driesdale happened to mention that I was particularly interested in athletic, young redheaded females.

The younger of the two said, "We can color our hair any color you wish!"

"Yes, yes, of course. Anything to please you."

Driesdale explained that I only like true, natural red hair.

The older woman, whom I felt was probably the madam of the service, said, "I do have one girl with strawberry-blond hair. Unfortunately, she is unavailable."

The conversation continued with various general topics being discussed. Driesdale brought the conversation back to the girl, innocently asking why she was unavailable.

The madam hesitated before answering, probably gauging if there was any risk involved in divulging the reason.

"She is in the hospital."

"Oh, I'm sorry, what happened?"

"One of her clients gave her a beating, she is in a pretty rough condition."

"Do you know who this client was?"

"No, I know not what he looks like, just that he is mean."

"Can we speak with her?"

"She is pretty badly beaten, I don't think . . ."

At this point, Driesdale outlined the reason that we were interested in speaking with the girl, that we must find this certain man. "Will she please help us?"

CHAPTER 65

Arrangements were eventually made to meet the next morning at a certain bistro. From there, the madam would take us to the hospital and the girl.

The hospital was small, and the girl was in their intensive care unit. She was indeed a strawberry blonde who had taken a severe beating. Her face was various shades of blue and purple, the swelling distorting her face grotesquely.

I felt my anger roiling up and threatening to spill out. I could not stand what had been done to this poor young woman. Driesdale began to speak with her after the madam had explained the reason for our visit. After about ten minutes, I noticed that the language had changed. I had no idea what they were saying or what language they were even speaking. The girl smiled faintly before visibly relaxing and conversing more openly. The madam and I left them alone while we sought out some coffee.

I learned later that the girl had been in the hospital for three to four days already, that it had been Grueber who had beaten her. The change in conversation had happened because she was actually Danish, and her Spanish was poor at the best of time. Driesdale had immediately picked up on her accent and told her some story about having a friend in a village not far from where she came from, hence her more relaxed state. He had put her more at ease by talking of familiar territory.

The only thing that was helpful to us was a passing comment by Grueber that, being the ultimate stud that he was, he was going to go where the real men play. Somehow, Driesdale deducted from this that Grueber was heading for Pamplona, where they have the famous running of the bulls.

The closest place that had any decent hotels was Murcia. We were in for a two–to three-day train ride across Spain.

CHAPTER 66

It was late afternoon when we came upon yet another dilapidated, run-down village in the middle of the jungle. This time, though, instead of waiting for darkness to fall, we went on ahead into the village. This was a change in the routine, so I put some effort into arousing myself back to reality. I had gotten so used to playing the crazy loon I found it difficult to drag myself back to sanity and actually remain sane. It requires a great deal more energy than I realized.

Almost immediately, I noticed a change in the general mood of the group. They seemed to perk up, taking more interest in their surroundings. They became serious and more focused, their body movements sharper as if there was suddenly a purpose. I wondered if maybe we had reached their home village or that they were at least known here.

The village itself, although appearing to be run-down, actually seemed to be the most modern that we had been in so far. It had power poles and lines crisscrossing the street.

The house that we entered was very much the same as all the previous ones that we had stayed in, but this one seemed to be more lived in. It looked like it was used more often. It wasn't as dusty or dirty. The furniture was in better shape. It even smelled like a house instead of a hovel. The walls were still stained and peeling but not quite as bad. I felt that this place was of some significance.

I was still weak and totally exhausted from my bout of fevered delirium. My body was grossly dehydrated, so much so that I had actually stopped sweating. When I peed, it was only a few painful drops. I now realized that they had been purposely keeping me on the brink of death for days now. I wasn't sure if that was a good sign or not. I still wasn't fully convinced that I would come out of this alive. Thinking did not help the continuous migraine that rumbled around my head. Sounds and light were magnified tenfold, making it feel like I was at a rock concert, standing next to the speakers. Sounds reverberated through my body, making it ache. I couldn't identify the different injuries anymore. It all made for one big pain. My skin hurt to touch it. So did my hair. A mere fly landing on my arm was agonizing and felt like a person was sitting there. I was struggling to swallow as my lips and tongue were so swollen. I could no longer chew the food that Maria would feed to me. She had begun to make some kind of gruel to feed me. At least this would slide down, only choking me now and then. I was surprised that my body was still functioning and that I was still coherent and conscious. Being half dragged, half carried was a nightmare for me. Just movement of any kind was torturous to my body.

After being thrown on the floor in my new private room, Maria came to feed me. Maria had to support me while I sipped on warm water and gruel. I couldn't taste anything, so it didn't really matter to me. I just knew that I had to take whatever nourishment was offered. My brain had taken over and had been in survival mode for some days.

Before leaving me for the night, Maria whispered in my ear that she would pray for me. That caused fear to tingle down my spine. It was confirmation that something was very different here.

CHAPTER 67

I don't know if I merely slept or just passed out, but I was grateful that I had been allowed to rest peacefully. I actually felt some benefit from being undisturbed, but again it was a change in routine, so I remained suspicious and uneasy about it. My fear and anxiety had subsided quite a bit once I had fallen into my role of the crazy, loony tune, but now its level was right back up there. Just the anticipation and not knowing was enhancing the anxiety and my imagination.

When Maria came in to feed me, her demeanor had changed too. She was serious and rigid in her body. She had a guard with her also. Gone was her faint smile that she reserved for me that encouraged me to hang in there.

In my weak raspy voice, I asked her what was going on. She just shook her head quickly, her eyes meeting mine, the expression on her face informing me, in a silent message, to stay quiet.

She was allowed to tell me that she could not tend to me as much as she had been. Her contact with me was to be kept to a bare minimum. The guard pulled her roughly up by her arm, and she willingly obeyed instead of showing the defiance that I had often seen her display.

I was ignored for the rest of the day. Even when passing by the door, no one would glance my way. This too became disturbing as the day wore on.

The house was a hive of frenzied activity, with many comings and goings in and out of the building. I heard a number of vehicles arrive and later leave, harsh words being exchanged between new voices outside. I could hear furniture being moved around in other rooms. Various boxes and containers were brought into the house while others would be taken out of the house.

Even the chief was acting differently. I actually at one point thought that he had finally lost it, gone over the edge. He was extremely manic, strutting and storming around the house, screaming orders and commands to his men. Suddenly he would stop dead in his tracks, halt his ranting, and appear to be listening to an unheard voice, only heard by him. He would nod his head as if agreeing before starting his frantic storming and ranting. He had a wild look in his eyes, becoming more and more agitated and animated. He would bark orders at his men, who were looking at him incredulously, not believing what had gotten into their leader. I think that he had suddenly woken up to the fact that he was among a bunch of low-functioning, bumbling baboons. His frustration with them being very apparent to anyone watching. On occasions, he would even strike out and slap or backhand his men around the head. It was hard to believe that the men that were scurrying around now were the same ones who had been so lax and laid back in the jungle. They too had fear in their eyes.

I was of the opinion that this was our final destination and that they were preparing for some event. I was convinced that it was my last few hours.

There was no frivolity or horseplay like there had been on all the previous nights. Everyone was subdued. Even the lively, loud, and raucous young women were quiet.

CHAPTER 68

We reached Murcia by midmorning. Both of us were anxious to get off the train and get to work. It had been a frustratingly long and boring journey. It had been annoying for both of us as we couldn't really make set plans as we didn't know what would be awaiting us in Murcia. Driesdale knew the area, no surprise there! Murcia had only three decent hotels to choose from. Anything less than a three-star rating was slumming it for Driesdale. He refused to stay in cheap accommodations.

It was always our policy whenever we traveled to not just book one hotel. We would always have at least two rooms in separate hotels. Nor would we enter or exit a taxi right outside the hotel. This way, we avoid being connected to any certain hotel.

We booked into all three of the bigger hotels.

We started our usual pattern of inquiries. The concierge proved to be very tight-lipped and of no use to us. We changed tactics and started to ask the bellhops, waiters, and maids. It didn't take long for a maid to recognize Grueber. She told us what room he was in, which happened to be on the fourth floor. All the rooms at the front of the hotel had balconies, offering a better view. She also told us that she was sure that he was still there.

Driesdale and I jumped into action immediately. We positioned ourselves at separate vantage points in the hotel so that we could observe all the traffic passing through the hotel. Driesdale was in the lobby, myself up on the rooftop with binoculars.

It was early evening when I saw a big blond-haired, handsome man exit a taxi and enter the hotel's front entrance. I immediately went to find Driesdale. We reached our room at the same time. Our adrenaline now coursing through our body, our thoughts on the blond man. We were certain that it was Grueber. It took us a while to track down the maid who had identified him as this was their quiet time of the day when they folded the clean linens and prepared for the next day. We eventually found her in a linen closet on the ground floor. We asked her if she would be willing to go to his door, knock, and say that she had a message to deliver. At first, she was adamant that she would not help. After all, she explained that it was not the normal time for the maids to be in the hallways. She was not comfortable with this plan at all. Driesdale used his powers of persuasion, and finally, she relented to us. Driesdale would accompany her to the door of the room. When the door opened, he would rush the door and tackle Grueber. We neglected to tell her this part of our plan. She just thought that Driesdale would be with her for support.

The old, ornate wrought iron elevator took forever to reach the fourth floor, where Driesdale and the maid got off. I carried on up to the next floor, where I had managed to obtain a room three doors down from his. I stationed myself on the balcony so that I could watch from the outside.

CHAPTER 69

As I was nervously waiting on the balcony a floor above where we thought that Grueber was, I suddenly heard three loud cracks, the unmistakable sound of gunfire. My stomach somersaulted as I wondered who fired and who got shot. As I was digesting these thoughts, I heard a distinctive clang outside. I was just in time to see Grueber swinging himself over his balcony and throwing himself onto the one below before breaking into the room.

Certain now that Driesdale was wounded or dead, I scrambled out of the room and made my way quickly to the floor below. My mind was racing with all sorts of scenarios that could greet me, but I was also very anxious not to let Grueber get away. We had him now.

I decided that the quickest way for me to get down to the fourth floor was to take the slow elevator; the emergency stairwell was too far out of my way.

When the door of the elevator opened, I had to go about thirty feet before turning a corner onto the hallway that held Grueber's room.

When I reached the door, the maid was lying dead in a pool of blood. Driesdale was already in the room, picking up bags that obviously belonged to Grueber. Time was all important now as shots had been fired, a maid was lying dead, and we knew that the police would be here any minute. Driesdale told me that Grueber was gone. We collected all the baggage and quickly made our way to the stairwell. We made it to the ground floor and found a service entrance where we exited onto an alley at the back of the hotel.

We grabbed a taxi and go to this café-bar combination that also rented rooms above. This was situated in the little village of Paloma. Once settled in the room, we started to sort through the bags to see if there was anything of use or interest. Driesdale recounted the scene back at the hotel. After the maid had knocked on the door and said that she had a message to deliver, the door opened abruptly as Grueber fired off his three shots. The first killing the maid, he then shot either side of the doorway in case there was anyone else there. Fortunately, Driesdale had the sense to stand to the side of the maid, out of sight to Grueber. He then turned and ran onto his balcony and made his escape.

Goddamit, we had lost him and had gotten an innocent person killed in the process.

The trail was now cold.

CHAPTER 70

Driesdale still had wood and paint chips in his hair from where the bullets had hit the doorframe.

Only clothes were contained in the baggage that we had taken from the room.

We had really botched this whole thing. We were a lot smarter than that and knew better. We had acted on the spur of the moment in reaction to a knee-jerk response. We had not thought anything through, had not followed my principle of the four Ps. We had just gone with an emotional response that had ended up in the shitter. It was just by luck that we had left no trace of us behind.

We also knew that the police would certainly now be looking for foreigners, not from Spain. We had to lie low for a while and plan our next move.

We had no clues, no information as to where on earth Grueber was heading. He knew none of the specifics, but he now knew that he was being pursued. Fortunately for us, he had not seen Driesdale back at the hotel.

As we sat around kicking ourselves in the butt, rehashing over and over the whole bungling farce, we couldn't decide on what our next move should be. One thing was for sure: we couldn't stay around here.

Out of the blue, Driesdale said, "Mrs. Johnson."

At first, I didn't comprehend what he was talking about. It took a few seconds to drag myself out of my self-pity party before I realized what he was on about.

Of course, Mrs. Johnson was an old friend of Driesdale who just so happened to be a psychic. I had met Mrs. Johnson on a few occasions when I had accompanied Driesdale to her grand dinner parties that she would hold.

He was of the opinion that she might very well be able to help us out. We had no other ideas at this time, so why not?

CHAPTER 71

Driesdale called her and gave her the tame version of our story before inquiring if she would be able to help us. They talked for a few minutes, he answering her various questions. In the end, she said that she wasn't getting anything from just talking to us, that we would have to send her his things. So we agreed to send her all of Grueber's belongings. We would call her back in a week.

Meanwhile, we had to decide where we were going to lie low. We didn't want to backtrack to any of the places that we had already visited, not a good thing to do in our business. We also had to choose a place where security wasn't so tight. We ended up deciding on Barcelona. We traveled by train from Murcia to Barcelona, where we waited to speak to Mrs. Johnson again. We knew that we definitely couldn't go walking around at night asking questions anymore. We had to sit tight and be patient.

Mrs. Johnson . . .

In the mid-1970s, Driesdale and I were traveling through Europe. We were in Germany. Driesdale wanted to make a detour as one of his friends was having a big dinner party. He wanted to go. I was happy to go along with him. He didn't mention where this party was, but a few train rides and connections later, I was surprised to find that we were in Zurich, Switzerland. We booked into a hotel, rented a car, and made our way to where the party was to be held on the outskirts of Zurich. I had to purchase a tuxedo, seeing that it was a black-tie deal. Of course, Mr. GQ Driesdale already had one.

Mrs. Johnson was in her midfifties, widowed, and of aristocratic stock. Her husband had been in international banking before he had died a number

154

of years ago. She lived comfortably in the country on an estate and had hired help to maintain the house and grounds.

As we began to drive up the gravel driveway, my mouth dropped in awe of this magnificent mansion, which was sitting nestled at the base of the mountains. The surroundings were truly breathtaking, and I realized that, for the first time, I could actually sit back and enjoy it, relaxing as we weren't on assignment.

Under the huge pillared portico of the "house," we stopped the car, and a valet took over. Upon entering the house, the lobby contained this enormous chandelier. It was the size of my apartment back home! Everything around me spoke of sheer, unadulterated opulence. We were greeted by a doorman, who relieved us of our coats. My amazement continued as we made our way into where there were about one hundred people. They were mingling and sipping champagne as they swapped pleasantries. Each room seemed to be bigger than my whole apartment building. It was truly magnificent and reminded me more of a palace than a mere mansion.

My attention was drawn to the most graceful woman that I had ever seen. She had blond hair and truly immaculate skin. She looked to be between forty or fifty years young. I assumed that she was the Mrs. Johnson. My thoughts were confirmed when she looked over to where Driesdale stood, and smiled. I was mesmerized. She reminded me of Grace Kelly the Hollywood actress.

We infused ourselves into the gathered crowd and ongoing polite conversation.

Most of the people spoke in broken English, which suited me, coming from Boston, as I too spoke broken English.

I was engaged in a conversation with this very haughty English banker and his wife.

"Do you know Mrs. Johnson?"

"No, actually my friend does."

"Oh, she's a very special lady."

"Yes, her beauty and elegance are arresting."

"No no, she has a very special talent. She's a psychic."

As I was learning this detail, Mrs. Johnson joined our little group.

"Our friend here is doubting your gift and abilities." He guffawed.

"No, it's not that I doubt your abilities, I have no experience in the area."

Mrs. Johnson gently took my arm. With a hint of her Danish accent, she said, "Let us take a walk."

She steered me willingly into this exceptionally large library. It had floor-to-ceiling glass doors that afforded you the opportunity to enjoy and take in the magnificent view of the mountains.

"You are not who you present yourself to be."

"There are a lot of us who have little secrets about us."

"But yours goes deeper than that."

A coy grin crossed my face as I replied, "I'm not all that deep."

She turned to face me. Taking both of my hands in hers, looking straight into my eyes, she said, "How are Gladys and Danny doing?"

I merely smiled. "They are doing well, thank you. I trust that you will be discreet in your conversations. I mean you no harm."

"Oh, I know. I've known Driesdale for many years and feel safe with him."

"Thank you. You are most gracious to open up your house to me."

"I believe that you are very good at what you do." The demure smile was still on her face.

"Well! I think that I need a drink now!"

She gently took my arm, and we returned to the party. How in the hell did she know the names of my parents? Not even Driesdale knew them.

That was how I first met Mrs. Johnson. A true lady.

CHAPTER 72

When a week was up, Driesdale again contacted her by phone.

At first, it seemed like we had hit a dead end. I could only hear our side of the conversation, and it didn't sound too promising. Then right at the end of the conversation, she said, "I see him in a cold climate. He's in a city. There are flowers in bloom."

"Anything more specific?"

"Something to do with him being at the international spy bottleneck of the world. That's all that I'm getting. I do hope that it helps you."

Driesdale thanked her for her time and help and ended the conversation. He had a big "I'm the cat that got the cream" grin on his face.

"What?" I asked.

"I do believe that I know what and where she speaks of."

"Which is . . . ?"

"I believe that our good friend Mrs. Johnson sees Grueber in Helsinki, Finland."

"How in the hell did you get that from what she said?"

"Helsinki, my friend, just happens to be the spy capital of the world. The majority of spy traffic at some time will pass through Helsinki. It is the current hub of all things illegal, whether it be diamonds, stolen art, human slaves, drugs, money laundering, you name it. All passes through there. It makes sense that he would choose Helsinki, he probably has a lot of contacts and informants there."

CHAPTER 73

Dawn came, and along with it came a new atmosphere. There was a sense of heightened tension in the air. Today, I was suddenly interesting again to everyone. It seemed as though they couldn't stop themselves from passing my door to take a peek.

I wondered what had happened to me overnight to suddenly recapture their attention.

Had all my wounds and injuries miraculously healed up? I shifted my body and found out that that was not the case. Had I suddenly sprouted wings and a halo? No, I knew that that would never happen! Stupid thought, John!

I had actually slept very well. I suspect I had been somewhat comatose through most parts of the night. I couldn't remember any dreams, nor could I remember anyone disturbing me during the night. I kind of felt somewhat refreshed. Hmm, odd.

Maria came in to feed me. Her demeanor remained the same as it had been the previous day, but I felt that she really wanted to tell me something. Again she had an escort who loomed over her, watching her every move. He had a mean, menacing glint in his eye. He hovered over her like a panther stalking its prey, ready to pounce at any second. What was with this dude? He was all gung ho and fired up, ready for action. Who had lit his fuse? Just as I was having that thought, Maria whispered, "Today . . ." Her sentence went unfinished as the guard swiftly smashed her in the side of her head, sending her sprawling across the floor. At that exact moment, the chief happened to be passing by my door and saw the whole exchange. In one swift movement, he had silently entered the room. Pulling a pistol from his side holster, he spun the unsuspecting guard around and fired. The guard's head snapped quickly back then forward again. The flat, empty eyes glazed as he momentarily remained standing before he crumpled to the floor. Staring at his face directly in front of me, a trickle of blood oozed its way out from the dark red hole in the center of his forehead. I recoiled in shock at what had just happened. The chief grabbed Maria's arm, hauling her to her unsteady feet before he shoved her out of the room. I remained unmoving on the floor as I tried to make sense of the scene that had just occurred.

In another room, I could hear the distinctive sound of four open-handed slaps delivered in rapid succession. Flesh on flesh. The blows maniacally dispatched. Faint whimpers escaping on gasping breath.

CHAPTER 74

My stomach surged as I felt the revulsion and bile rising in my throat. The stench of new death filtering to my nostrils. I actually started to retch, at the same time desperately trying to hold on to my meager breakfast.

Two guards silently entered the room, a sense of horror suddenly washing over me.

Gently, they picked me up, carrying me between them. They took me into another room.

They set me down in a high-backed wooden chair before tying my hands to the arms.

I scanned the room slowly as I took in its contents. I was alone.

The room definitely had that more lived-in feel to it. There were real drapes to the window instead of the usual tattered, rotting scraps of fabric at other houses. There was a well-worn but relatively clean-looking rug on the floor. The desk actually had papers and various sundry items on it and was free of dust. I had definitely come up in this degenerated part of the world.

Then I spotted the telephone sitting proudly alone on a side table. A thin stream of sunlight was cheekily peeping through a narrow gap in the drapes and was highlighting it. "Ta-da! Here I am."

After a while, Maria came into the room to give me a drink. This time she was alone.

I asked her why she didn't leave.

"I cannot."

"Why? Why do you stay with such cruel people?"

"My husband."

"What, they've got him captive somewhere?"

"No, no. He here," she said as she fed me more of the cool liquid. I knew it wasn't water even though I couldn't taste it. I had a sudden thought that it was poison or something. I tried pulling away from her. She saw my sudden fear.

"It okay. It good, it help you. My husband." She motioned to the chief as he passed the doorway.

"Whaat! You're not serious?"

"*Sí*. He take me from my family when I young girl."

This information completely blew my mind before it just served to exacerbate my existing hatred and disgust that I felt toward the little piss ant. Everything now seemed to be very confusing. I was alarmed at their sudden concern for me. My thoughts began to bounce around in my head, making me even more paranoid than I already was. It wasn't poison, but maybe it was laced with something to drug me, to put me out. It was Maria's only way of helping me to go quietly.

"S' okay," she said as she left the room.

My paranoia had returned at warp speed. I found myself questioning everything, their every move, every action, every word. I couldn't trust them. I was even beginning to doubt Maria. Maybe she had had an actual part in my execution. I sat there waiting for the concoction to take effect, all these thoughts reeling around in my mind.

CHAPTER 75

We had decided that Amsterdam was a safe bet as we made our way across Europe to our new destination of Helsinki. Some countries were safe in that they didn't monitor the traffic passing through their country. Others were to be avoided like the clap, especially if you were doing what we were. Amsterdam was also known for its illegal trade traffic, having quite the reputation among those of us who moved within the underground world. Security checkpoints were few and far between, the authorities friendly and often helpful. Such nice people.

The flight to Helsinki was terrifying, to say the least. I think that we must have passed through hell to get there.

The flight passed over the Baltic Sea. A sea that is ruthless and unforgiving even in the height of summer.

To Driesdale's disgust, we had decided that it be wiser to travel economy class so that we would blend in better and were therefore less likely to attract attention to ourselves. What a nightmare! The plane was continuously buffeted by high gale-force winds. The turbulence kept us bobbing up and down like a dinghy in the height of a storm.

The cramped economy section was crammed to capacity with a mixture of businessmen and families. The narrowness and hardness of the seats only added to our discomfort.

A baby was wailing somewhere behind us, and children whimpered as their parents could only look on sheepishly while trying desperately to reassure them with false and empty statements that even they didn't believe themselves.

The stewardesses were harried as they tried desperately but unsuccessfully to calm their passengers. Vodka was being served by the bucketful, with people gulping it down much quicker than they usually would. I believe that some were even scared that the vodka would run out before they had attained their state of drunken stupor. Most of the passengers were quiet, sitting nervously, awaiting the pending disaster. Some were actually puking from the bouncy ride. The sound of retching echoed throughout the plane. I found myself having to gulp hard in order to hold on to the contents of my stomach. The pungent stench of vomit emanating through the air. Some people were hiding behind the bravado of forced nervous laughter in an attempt to hide their terror.

I actually offered up a prayer that we would at least arrive in one piece.

We made it and quickly set about checking in to three hotels in the different parts of the city of Helsinki.

We were confident that Grueber was going to be around somewhere.

Our intentions were to sleep during the day, doing our hunting/searching by night. Our awareness was at 110 percent. The closer we felt that we were to Grueber, the more care and attention we had to pay.

This time, we would make sure to use the four Ps!

CHAPTER 76

On our second night of prowling the bars, we came across this bustling basement bar.

Driesdale was reluctant to go inside. I plagued him in my smart-ass fashion.

"What's the matter, frightened of catching something? You won't catch anything if you don't touch anything!"

"Funny. Ha-ha. We need to stick to our plan."

"But we are. I think this could be a useful place."

We descended the stone steps and entered into the bar. After pausing a minute to acclimate our eyes to the dim lighting, it was easy to see that it was not quite what we were expecting it to be. The room was no bigger than one of those high-rent but minute apartments that you find in New York City.

As we made our way through the crowded tables. Cutting through the layers of heavy smoke, we found ourselves bumping against fishermen, soldiers, and cheap bawdy whores looking for their next fare. We found ourselves in this seedy, overcrowded, and raucous smoke-filled den of lowlifes. Just as this dawned on me, this drunken, what I assumed to be fisherman almost knocked me over as he staggered into me.

"Sorry, it's awfully crowded in here." He was to have none of it. Maybe he didn't understand me. Driesdale apologized for me in their native tongue. Still, the man was obviously spoiling for a rumble. This was all we needed. Might as well shine the spotlight on us now!

"Let's get out of here," I said over my shoulder to Driesdale, who immediately nodded his agreement. When I attempted to pass by the fisherman, he stepped in my path and pulled a knife. The lengthy blade becoming an extension of his hand. Him being as loaded as he was, was thankfully to my advantage. He was staggering pretty badly, barely able to

stand. Deciding to act immediately, I tensed my right arm, making my hand into a fist as I swung it down like a pendulum sweeping away anything in its path. I pivoted on my left foot as I brought my right leg around to drive my foot into his ample gut. He grunted as he toppled backward, landing on his back on the floor. We made a swift exit.

I really doubted that the police would be showing up anytime soon to an establishment the likes of this one.

CHAPTER 77

There wasn't a great deal said between us once we had gotten back to one of the hotel rooms.

"Nice one."

"Yeah, it's not what I thought it was. I don't know what I was thinking."

"It's generally difficult to be able to think when one's head is up one's ass."

End of conversation. Hidden reprimand duly noted!

On our fourth night of hunting, we happened upon this high-class, fancy bar with a huge lounge.

"More like it," came Driesdale's dry comment.

Making ourselves comfortable at one of the many plush seating arrangements, I sat with my back to the room while Driesdale sat facing the bar. Behind his head was a huge glass-fronted picture in a gilt frame. It actually afforded me a pretty good view of the room reflected behind me. The bar was in an S shape.

Sitting there casually chatting and watching the various traffic pass through, I noticed this stunningly beautiful redhead at the bar tolerating two guys who had neglected to wear their drool bibs. It was obvious that she had no interest in them.

In my best casual manner, I turned around as if I was studying the various art displayed on the walls. I took a glance at the redhead, hoping that I had not been obvious.

Driesdale gave me a mildly questioning look.

"The stunning redhead at the bar . . ."

"Yes, I've been watching her. A most beautiful creature."

"Yes, but have you noticed the bruise on her cheek that her carefully applied makeup has failed to hide?"

"I have indeed."

Trying to come up with a way to get her away from the two morons, we sat there contemplating different options. We decided that the only way to get her attention would be to pass her a note via the waiter. Driesdale scribbled a note on a paper napkin and waved the waiter over to us.

As luck would have it, at that precise moment, one of the morons got up and left, presumably to use the bathroom. Driesdale seized the opportunity and asked the waiter to deliver the note. The content of the note being that Driesdale had offered to buy her a drink on my behalf. Me being the painfully shy person that I am.

Upon receiving the note, she looked over in our direction, a smile playing on her lips. Getting smoothly out of her seat, she slowly slinked her way around the room before placing herself right next to Driesdale.

I remembered my manners by not drooling. Up close, she was truly exquisite.

Driesdale began the conversation in Finnish. It seemed awkward at the start, then the language changed. I thought that I detected a few Russian words in there. I was correct. Her name was Tatiana; she was Russian. Driesdale put her at ease by speaking to her in her native dialect, giving her some story about knowing someone in the village where she was from. He didn't know someone, of course. This was how he disarmed people. Driesdale told her that we just wanted to talk. She said that she didn't do two on one. "Fine," said Driesdale. "Let's go somewhere quiet where we can talk." Before they left, she excused herself to go to the ladies' room.

We discussed the plan of action. If he should get some good information from her, he should arrange for her to set up a meeting with Grueber and meet her again the following day to get the details. They left to go to one of our other hotels.

CHAPTER 78

I didn't end up passing out or falling unconscious.

After some time passed, the chief, Maria, Brutus, and a couple of guards entered the room, and I couldn't believe what I was seeing.

Every one of them was standing straighter, taller. Their clothes were cleaner, along with their faces. Their unruly hair was combed and in place. And most unnerving of all, the chief was smiling.

Oh, mother of God, help me, he has finally lost it!

As the guards untied my wrists, the chief placed the side table with the phone on it in front of me. And he was still smiling.

I hope that I'm reading him correctly!

The chief placed another chair at ninety degrees to me on my right. Brutus was standing to my immediate left. Once again his foul, fetid breath started to tickle my nostrils, causing me to have to breathe through my mouth.

How was it possible that he was so healthy with all that decay and infection in his mouth? A normal person would have died long ago.

Maria took her seat and looked at me. A smile of encouragement flickered across her face.

Trying to focus clearly on the task at hand, I had to push all the pain out of my mind.

The chief pointed to the phone. "Call."

Nodding, I picked up the handset. Once again Maria would do the dialing. My coordination was out of control. My body was trembling internally, and I just hoped that it was not showing on the outside.

I recited the number to myself a couple of times to make sure that I got it right.

Maria leaned toward me. "This has to go good."

"I know." I took a slow, deep breath before I began to tell her the numbers.

The chief suddenly started to shout, asking why I took so long, and began to pace rapidly back and forth in front of us.

Concentrating really hard, feeling dizzy again, I fought to remain focused.

The numbers were dialed. It starts to ring. Then the unthinkable happened. A recorded voice came on the line. "Your call cannot be completed as dialed. Please check the number and try again." *Oh. My. God. I'm dead.*

My facial expression must have been what set the chief off as all of a sudden he was screaming, his face ashen, his hair now disheveled, sweat pouring down his face, his eyes wild and on fire. Instant lunatic.

CHAPTER 79

My thoughts were suddenly confirmed and seemed to be about to take place as he took his gun from its holster at his side. His hand moved swiftly as he brought the revolver in front of his face. Everyone was frozen in place, nobody expecting this. The scene stood still. All eyes were on the madman with the gun. A cold sweat trickled its way down my spine.

He looked at the gun momentarily, as if he didn't quite know what it was, before he quickly pointed it into my face. All three of us moved simultaneously. Brutus dove to his left. Maria dove behind and to her right, knocking over her chair as she scrambled out of the way. I tried to dive to my right but only managed to flop off the chair onto my hip and shoulder, spinning on the rug as my legs attempted to kick and gain traction. I was now a deer caught in the headlights as I looked into the eyes of a madman.

Awaiting his next move, my body was screeching out in pain at the fall I had just taken. Dizziness threatened to render me unconscious. Squeezing my eyes closed, I tried to refocus.

I drew in some ragged breaths, desperately trying to control the trembling that had suddenly seized the outside of my entire body. If I hadn't been so dehydrated, I believe that I would have peed my pants.

Replacing his gun back in its holster, he motioned for me to try the phone again.

This time, we stayed on the floor. After composing myself, I repeated the sequence of numbers, and Maria dialed them.

It rang . . . and rang . . . and it rang.

Once I heard the connection being made, I didn't wait for an answer from the other end. I blurted out my words as quickly as I could.

"Uncle John! Where are we at?"

"Johnny, it's so good to hear from you. Are you all right?

"Yeah, just a little tired is all."

"It's been three days since I last heard from you. What is the holdup?"

I knew that I had to try to keep him on the phone for at least five minutes so that they could try to trace the call. The chief was back to his screaming and pacing. I turned my back to him to try to hear what Uncle John was saying. He made a grab for the handset, but I blocked him with my body. He was screaming something about there being only one chopper. I raised my finger to try to tell him to give me a minute to arrange the details, but he was on me like a wolf on a rabbit. I finally told Uncle John that I couldn't hear him and if he would please talk to this crazy son of a bitch. He agreed. I paused before I handed over the phone, just long enough for the chief to recheck himself and calm down.

He snatched the handset out of my hand, picked up the cradle of the phone, and walked to the far side of the room.

Maria's eyes were reflecting the terror that was surging through my mind.

CHAPTER 80

As I sat trying to regain control and calm my body and mind, I could make out some of the details that the now calm chief was talking of.

I caught mention of only one chopper, in a field, some miles away. The money was to be dropped in a bag with a radio in it. If everything was in order, then the exchange would take place. The conversation and negotiations lasted for a while longer. Then everyone left me by myself lying on the rug on the floor.

I wasn't totally convinced that this was going to happen, with all sorts of crazy wild thoughts ricocheting around my head, let alone that Uncle John would keep his word and help me. I couldn't see how it would go smoothly since it seemed that the chief had abruptly lost his mind. It was a terrifying thought to think that he was in charge.

Maria brought me my food and a drink. She confirmed the negotiated details. It did nothing to convince me that (a) the exchange would happen, (b) I would get rescued, and (c) they would not kill me before the money was dropped.

Despite all the wild celebrations that were occurring throughout the house, I was left feeling very skeptical about the whole business. I fully believed that I wouldn't make it through the night.

CHAPTER 81

The arrangement was that Driesdale would meet her the next day at 10:00 a.m.

She confirmed that it was Grueber that had put his mark on her. Driesdale had had a hell of a time convincing her to help us out by meeting once more with Grueber. She was terrified of the man and wanted nothing more to do with him. He finally persuaded her by telling her that Grueber was a killer. A brutal man who must be found before he killed again. That we had been hunting him for some time as he had killed and hurt people so very dear to us.

She informed Driesdale that Grueber would only entertain the ladies in his own hotel suite. He would never just meet them and go to a place. This was a problem, but one that we could work around.

While Driesdale went to meet with Tatiana, I went to meet my new friend. I went shopping for my weapon. A rifle with scope, of course. My cover story was that I was going to do some elk hunting.

When we meet up later in our room, Driesdale had Grueber's hotel and room number. Tatiana would be spending the night with him two nights from now.

Time was short, so we had to carry out our four Ps to the nth degree.

Early the next day, we went to the hotel that Tatiana had told us that Grueber was staying in. While Driesdale went to find and bribe a maid to go into Gruber's suite and to just stand in the bedroom window, I was busy being on the roof of the building directly opposite. I needed to see exactly which his room was before I could sight in my scope. It took up most of the afternoon to do so. I had to be so precise and accurate. I knew that this was our only chance and that I had to get it right. Like the marine snipers say, "One bullet, one kill."

Our anxiety levels were running sky-high at this point. Both of us deeply concentrating on our own individual tasks, replaying the scene over and over in our minds.

We didn't speak. There was this shared but accepted tension in the air.

Of course, I was afraid. All manner of things could go wrong. Timing was of the essence, only having that narrow window of opportunity to work with.

That night, we ordered up room service. We didn't want to be distracted at this time. We still had many hours to go before it went down. The immense amount of pressure I felt was causing my head to pound. Everything was riding on my performance.

The next day, we meet up again in the afternoon. Driesdale again bribed the same maid, only this time to actually let us into his room. Driesdale had spent the morning in the hotel lobby watching for Grueber, while I had been making sure that my position on the roof was secure.

We entered the room. I placed a timer on the lamp by the right side of the bed. This was the closest lamp to the window. I also slid the side table closer to the window so that you would have to actually get up to shut it off.

Driesdale finagled with the drapes and fixed them so that they would not close all the way across the window.

We had prearranged with Tatiana that at 3:00 a.m. the timer would make the light come on. She had to make sure that Grueber was on the right side of the bed. Her instructions were to be very compliant with Grueber—have an early dinner, cater to his every whim, and get him loaded so that he would hopefully pass out.

CHAPTER 82

We knew what time Tatiana was meeting Grueber at his hotel. We were in position on the rooftop opposite way ahead of that time. We were both sweating, feeling the pressure build. I really had to rein in and put away my feelings regarding the task at hand. Driesdale calmly and quietly talked to me. It helped to keep me calm and focused.

It was a chilly night, in the low fifties despite it being summertime. We were now avid clock watchers, willing the time away.

After a couple of hours had passed, we saw the lights go on in Grueber's suite. It was around the same time that we had estimated they would reach the room.

As instructed, we watched as Tatiana switched on the lamp by the bed. As the night wore on, we started to sweat as the time crept closer and closer to our 3:00 a.m. deadline.

Finally, after apparently having a long roll in the hay, the lights were turned off in the suite. The time was about 1:30 to 1:45 a.m. That was cutting it close.

At 3:00 a.m. sharp, the lamp was turned on by the timer. I was ready and watching through the scope. Sure enough, Grueber got out of bed to shut off the lamp.

Inhaling deeply yet slowly, I stopped midbreath, and I fired. I continued to watch as the scene played out through my scope. I saw Grueber's body jerk before he fell to the floor, screaming. I allowed a faint smile to play on my lips. I was satisfied, and I dropped the rifle.

"You fucker, you fucking missed him on purpose." Driesdale was enraged, believing I would do such a thing. I quickly calmed him down, asked him what hotel he would go to. I told him that I would call him.

It took me a few minutes to enter the hotel and reach the room.

I knew that I had wounded Grueber badly. I had crippled him with the shot to his spine.

I knew that he wouldn't function as well as he had a minute or two earlier.

CHAPTER 83

When I entered the room, Tatiana was crying and whimpering, cowering in a corner. I quickly gathered her clothes and, as I handed them to her, told her to get out of there.

She didn't need telling twice. The shock and terror visible in her eyes.

Grueber was lying half propped up on his side, trying to reach for a gun hidden under the mattress.

I leaped over to him and stepped on his throat. I could see that he was bleeding profusely. I replaced my foot with a knife and held it so that it was poking into his skin over his carotid artery. A small trickle of blood escaped from where the point of the knife had broken the skin over his carotid artery.

I held a picture of Marylyn in front of his face.

"You met her in Prague," I growled.

"I don't remember, I have many women in many places."

Neither one of us was to be trusted; we both knew that.

I showed the bloodstained once-green scapular to him, saying, "You left this driven into her forehead. I can promise you that whatever you do or don't remember on your journey to hell, I can promise you that the last thing that you will remember is my eyes."

With that, I grabbed him at the back of his head by his pretty boy blond hair. I plunged the knife into his neck on his left side and then gave two good tugs of the blade so that it splayed open his throat. His carotid artery was slit, and so was his esophagus. He rasped as he quickly bled to death. I released the knife, got to my feet, and briskly walked away.

It was like treading on a cockroach. It's messy, and it makes a sound, but you just keep on walking. I didn't consider its family or children.

Grueber died the way that he lived. Cold and unemotionally.

I was devoid of feeling. I felt no remorse. I felt no relief. I just wanted to get it done.

It was done.

CHAPTER 84

I could fight no longer. The pain had finally overwhelmed me. My vision was a total blur, my sense of survival totally drained. There was nothing left. I hurt, oh my god, I hurt.

They had left me. The peace would come quickly now. The darkness could finally embrace me to its bosom. My pain would be taken away. I felt nothing. All was black.

I was with Marylyn in bed. We were lying on our sides, facing each other and smiling.

"You'll be all right."

I was puzzled. I didn't understand.

"You'll be all right," she said again before she disappeared.

The next thing I knew was that the blackness returned, and I heard Marylyn shouting my name and that I had to wake up.

CHAPTER 85

I slowly stirred out of the mind-numbing stupor that I had allowed myself to fall into. I realized an odd thing. It was quiet. No night insect noises were filtering through the window down the hall. No voices, laughter, or sounds of movement. No noises. It was very quiet. Eerily quiet. Not a sound. Silence.

The silence captured my attention. I was now awake.

Straining to listen for any sound, I heard the occasional faint grunts, groans, belches, and snores of people sleeping in the next room. They have partied themselves into oblivion.

My battered and broken body remained where I was thrown on the filthy wood floor in the darkened room. The reek of old death and years of filth emanated from the stained floor inches from my face. The bugs continued to dine on my skin, the relentless smothering heat weighing like a wet wool blanket over my body. As exhausted as I was, I was unable to shift positions to better see my surroundings. I didn't really care anymore.

The light cast from the other room down the hall made it possible for me to make out the silhouette of the man standing guard inside the front door. An AK-47 was casually slung over his shoulder. He was sleeping on his feet.

I jolted as a loud crack hit the front door, exploding it open just as the guard dropped to the floor. He was dead.

Automatic gunfire exploded around me. In the darkness, the muzzle flashed, and earsplitting noise from the AK-47s made it confusing as to who was shooting whom. There was screaming and shouting in Spanish, the sound of people scurrying around trying to dodge the bullets. The alcohol was making their reactions slow.

Among the riot of noise, I saw this guy coming toward me. He looked like one of those Delta Force motherfuckers, dressed all in black; even his face was black.

I started shouting as best as I could, "I'm the prize. I'm the American rich kid. I'm the prize. I'm the prize."

As he untied me, he said, "You don't look like much of a prize, son."

"I don't much feel like one."

Dragging me to my feet, he started to drag me toward the door. Among all the chaos around me, my heart stuttered a few beats as I saw a woman come running around the corner. It was Maria. She stopped in her tracks.

"Wait, no, wa . . ." My words died in my throat as she was gunned down. As I watched her body crumple to the floor, I counted at least six bullet wounds slowly making their bloody marks on her clothes. I couldn't do anything to stop it. I couldn't believe it. She shouldn't have been shot. She was kind to me. I was gutted.

I tried to make a move over to where she was now lying. I got yanked in the opposite direction, away from her.

"Come on, man, we've gotta get out of here. And I mean now!"

Once outside, I was bundled into the bed of some old pickup truck. The driver gunned the engine, wheels spinning and kicking up dirt as we screeched down the road.

I was trying to sit up and get my bearings. The truck swerved into what appeared to be an open field area. A chopper was waiting, with its rotors still running, the pilot frantically waving us over. I was carried across the dirt and thrown into the chopper. We immediately became airborne.

Everything had happened so suddenly, the entire operation lasting for maybe five minutes, beginning to end.

I lay where I landed, trying to sort out my mind. The pilot turned to me and said, "You must know some very important people. We've been through a lot to get you out."

I replied, "No, it's not a case of who you know but what you know."

CHAPTER 86

As prearranged, I called Driesdale at his hotel. He was still angry at me.
"Did you complete the job?"
"Yes."
"I'm sure that you are very happy now."
"No. I'm not happy. I'm not anything. What's done is done. It needed to be done. It's over with."

We caught the same flight to London, England, but we didn't fly together.
We met up as prearranged.
"You know that they'll never let us work together again."
"I know that. They will act out, dish up their punishment. You are a company man, you should be all right. They'll probably assign you to a desk job while they evaluate your stability. That isn't an option for me. I'm just a contract, spare parts."
"We didn't actually do anything to embarrass anybody."
"No, but we sure pissed them off."
"I guess I'll head back to the States. I'll place an ad in the personal section of the *New York Times* to let them know that we are back from our vacation."
I knew that that would be the last time that I would ever see Driesdale again. I was a dead man walking. I was the target now.
"Please take care, and do what you need to do to stay safe." My words catching in my throat.
"What about you?"
"I'll do the same. I'm better now, my head is clear again. I'll just face whatever presents itself. I can't keep on like this."
We gave each other a hug before we turned and walked in different directions.

EPILOGUE

PART 1

I flew to Shannon Airport on the outskirts of Limerick, Ireland.

I had old friends there that I could stay with for a while.

John and Mary O'Toole were good Irish people. They had two children.

John was a mechanic who worked on motors and compressors in the shipyards. They knew not to ask questions.

One day, while they were all out–John at work, Mary and the kids shopping–I wrote them a long letter.

I told them in the letter that they would most likely never see me again. I wasn't going to go into details as I didn't want to put their safety in jeopardy.

I thanked them for their help and friendship over the years. I enclosed five thousand English pounds.

Shamus was their huge Irish wolfhound. He had never been too fond of me, always growling when our paths crossed.

He kept staring at me the entire time that I was writing that letter.

"Take care of John, Mary, and the kids for me. I won't be coming back."

He walked over to me and just placed his head in my lap. He understood.

"Oh, damn you! I've lived in fear of you all these years." I bent to kiss him on his big block of a head. Then I left.

It was a very somber three weeks for me. It was also extremely difficult for me to accept that I would never see them again. I struggled with that for a long time.

PART 2

The Pan Am flight to New York was to be a nine-hour flight. As I was settling into my seat in coach class, a stewardess approached me. She said that there were some empty seats in first class and asked if I would like to move.

A huge sickening wave of déjà vu hit me like a ton of bricks as I had a flashback to Marylyn.

My voice cracked as I fought back tears. "No, I'm fine right here. Thank you for the offer."

My frame of mind was somber, almost morbid, as I realized just what I might be facing back in the States. I was still grieving the recent loss of some very significant people in my life and wasn't feeling too optimistic about my future.

Nine hours is a long time to sit by yourself, contemplating what comes next. I repeatedly weighed what I saw were my options.

I knew that I had made a mistake. I had stepped out of the zone, turning the whole affair from what was business into something very personal. It had meant something to me, something that I couldn't just block out and disassociate myself from in order to take care of business.

It was much like standing on a crack in the ice. You are always wondering when it will get bigger, and you will fall through. Nobody has the answers.

I finally decided where I needed to be in the world, and it felt like a very lonely place.

I had taken the oath to never betray my country, and I still honor that.

The idea of freelancing for some mercenary company had been tossed around as one of the options. I had had enough of that whole scene.

I would return to the United States to face the consequences. Whatever I did, I knew that I was fucked anyway.

It was during the flight and all of my reflecting that I recalled the first time that I had met John O'Toole.

I was sitting in a little pub on the grounds of Belfast Airport. I was killing time between connections to New York. I was drinking soda as I was on assignment. I was talking to the barman when a guy sitting three stools down also joined the conversation.

"Do you pass through here often then?"

"Oh, a few times a year, now and then when I'm on business."

He went on to tell me that he traveled also. He worked in Belfast in the shipyards but lived just outside of Limerick. His work sometimes took him around the country.

A while later, as we walked out of the pub together, two thugs approached and started to give John O'Toole a hard time.

I made some casual comment to one of them, to which he replied, "You need to go back from where ye come from while you still can."

Taking a step closer to test his bravado, I said, "Really?"

As he drew his clenched fist back, winding up to plant one on me, I swiftly filled the gap between us and jabbed him hard in the throat. He dropped to the floor. His partner quickly departed.

"Geez, John. You sure make friends easily."

"They are no friends of mine. I need to call the wife. I don't get to call often as it's expensive."

"Well, here, let me help you out." I offered a handful of coins out to him.

"Ohh, I canye let you do that."

I insisted and ended up feeding the pay phone God knows how many coins. He spoke with his wife before he put me on the phone with her.

"John tells me that ye helped him with a spot o' bother earlier. I thank ye fer that."

They extended an invitation to me that the next time that I was in the area, that I was to call them and stop by to see them.

I called them about six months later. I rented a car, got lost, had to call him five times along the way before he drove to come and meet me.

John O'Toole and his wife, Mary, had two children, also called John and Mary. They had an Irish wolfhound called Shamus.

As the years went on, they were very gracious to let me stay with them. John was tall, lean, and had a ruddy complexion. Mary was a true mother hen, down to earth and sweet. Shamus hated me.

I would convalesce there between assignments. It was so beautiful where they lived. So peaceful.

We had this mutual suspicion between us that neither one of us were what we said we were. We never questioned each other.

PART 3

At Kennedy airport, I stopped at a newsstand. It was a Sunday in New York. I asked the guy if he had a copy of yesterday's *New York Times*.

"Yeah, sure, I got one lying around here. You can have it. It's old news anyway."

I opened it to the classified section. I scanned down the personal ads.

There it sat quite simple and to the point.

> JB
> The family is having a reunion.
> Please let us know if you can attend.
> Uncle John.

It was a message meant for me.

Edwards Brothers Malloy
Thorofare, NJ USA
January 29, 2013